# PREVIOUS BOOKS BY ALAN REFKIN

## Fiction

**Matt Moretti and Han Li Series**
*The Archivist*
*The Abductions*
*The Payback*
*The Forgotten*

**Mauro Bruno Detective Series**
*The Patriarch*
*The Scion*
*The Artifact*
*The Mistress*

**Gunter Wayan Series**
*The Organization*
*The Frame*
*The Arrangement*

## Nonfiction

*The Wild Wild East: Lessons for Success in Business in Contemporary Capitalist China*
By Alan Refkin and Daniel Borgia, PhD

*Doing the China Tango: How to Dance around Common Pitfalls in Chinese Business Relationships*
By Alan Refkin and Scott Cray

*Conducting Business in the Land of the Dragon: What Every Businessperson Needs To Know About China*
By Alan Refkin and Scott Cray

*Piercing the Great Wall of Corporate China: How to Perform Forensic Due Diligence on Chinese Companies*
By Alan Refkin and David Dodge

# THE CABAL

## A **MATT MORETTI** AND **HAN LI THRILLER**

ALAN REFKIN

# THE CABAL
## A MATT MORETTI AND HAN LI THRILLER

iUniverse books may be ordered through booksellers or by contacting:

iUniverse
1663 Liberty Drive
Bloomington, IN 47403
www.iuniverse.com
844-349-9409

ISBN: 978-1-6632-4528-1 (sc)
ISBN: 978-1-6632-4527-4 (e)

Library of Congress Control Number: 2022917073

Print information available on the last page.

iUniverse rev. date:   09/12/2022

To my wife, Kerry
To Ed Houck

# PROLOGUE

*July 5, 2008—5:15 a.m.* in Musa Qala, *Helmand Province, Afghanistan*

The approach of the CH-47 Chinook helicopter into Musa Qala wasn't subtle. At one hundred twenty decibels, the noise produced by the twin-engine, tandem-rotor aircraft could be heard from six miles away. The provincial governor, Nadir Ahmadzai, and five of the town's elders looked north and saw it as a speck near the three thousand five hundred feet mountains to the west. Not wanting to appear overanxious, they stepped back inside the mud-brick structure, which served as the provincial seat of government, and waited for the foreigners to arrive. As they sat around a weathered rectangular table and drank tea, the rhythmic noise of the helicopter's engines got louder and the speck transformed into the profile of the Chinook, which was now less than a mile away. That's when it happened.

Had Ahmadzai and the elders remained outside the mud-brick structure, they would have seen a streak of fire race from a patch of ground three-quarters of a mile in front of them and strike the rear of the aircraft, blowing it out of the sky. The attack surprised the governor because he'd ordered every person in the province not to fire any weapon from sunrise to sundown, long after the helicopter was scheduled to depart. When he heard the explosion in the distance, he was furious that someone had violated his proclamation. Pushing his chair away from the table, scraping its ancient legs on the equally old wooden floor, he stood to go outside to see if he could spot the offender who'd fired the weapon. That was as far as he got before the mud brick building disintegrated in a fiery blast, instantly killing him and the elders.

There were eleven souls onboard the Chinook—seven Army Rangers and a flight crew of four. Five of the seven died when a shoulder-fired Chinese FN-6 missile slammed into the aircraft's aft rotor, sending pieces of it through the rear fuselage. The four-person crew was killed when the aircraft violently impacted the ground nose-first. The Ranger team's commander, Captain Matthew Moretti, who was in the first seat directly behind the cockpit, survived but broke his back, the impact rendering him unconscious. The second survivor, Captain Douglas Cray, the regiment intelligence officer, was seated to his right. He had just unfastened his five-point harness to retrieve his briefcase when the missile struck and was jettisoned out the opening where the M134D minigun was mounted when the aircraft crashed. Although he hit the ground hard, he escaped with only scrapes and bruises.

With the aft end of the wreckage in flames and the fire moving forward, Cray knew it wouldn't be long before it reached the fuel tanks, which lined both sides of the forward fuselage. Wanting to get anyone who survived out of the aircraft, he rushed into the darkened interior through the opening where he was ejected. Checking the cockpit first, he saw that both pilots and the two crew members seated behind them, who were all still buckled into their seats, were lifeless—entangled in the jagged pieces of wreckage that had impaled them. Quickly turning to look at the interior of the broken fuselage, he could see the flames were rapidly growing in intensity and moving towards him. Had it not been for the glow of that fire, he might have missed Moretti, whose seat had broken loose and was partially hidden behind a jagged piece of fuselage.

As Cray started towards him, the interior became a shooting gallery as ammunition began to ignite, randomly sending bullets in every direction. Quickly unstrapping Moretti, he dragged the burly two hundred thirty pounds, six feet, three inches tall Ranger out the minigun opening as projectiles bounced off the steel interior around them. Once clear, and with no idea if Moretti was dead or alive, he put him into a firefighter's carry and tried to get as far from the Chinook as possible. With the burly Ranger as dead weight, he could only get thirty yards from the wreckage before the forward fuel tanks exploded—the blast force slapping them to the ground as several large pieces of metal streaked overhead, accompanied by a wave of searing heat. When he turned to look at the aircraft, he saw that half the fuselage was missing.

Cray's face was singed from the searing heat of the blast as he turned Moretti on his back and laid him flat to see if he was alive or if he'd been carrying a corpse. Finding that he was breathing, he reached into his heavily soiled uniform and pulled out his satphone, calling the operations center at Bagram Air Base, three hundred miles away. Although he didn't know his coordinates, they told him that the Chinook's emergency locator transmitter activated on impact and transmitted its location. "We'll be there in two hours. Hang in there," base ops replied.

"I'm not sure we'll live that long. We're attracting a crowd," Cray countered, seeing a dozen Afghans with guns coming towards them.

"A medevac and a rescue team with significant firepower are on their way. We'll monitor the GPS coordinates from your satphone. Keep it on and with you. If you're captured, we'll know where they've taken you."

Cray ended the call and put the satphone in his pocket, wanting to keep it out of sight.

As he looked at the approaching crowd of Afghans, he saw the focused, determined looks on their faces. From how they held their weapons, he knew that years of fighting had hardened these men. The person leading them was of medium height, had a gray beard, and walked with a limp. Because of his age and that everyone walked half a step behind, he assumed this person was the senior elder, which meant the others would defer to his judgment.

The purpose of his visit was to sign an understanding between the provincial governor and the United States government to bring peace to one of the most lawless areas in the country. Someone thought that agreement was a bad idea and decided to blow his helicopter out of the sky. With the smoking remains of the Chinook behind him, he believed those approaching belonged to whatever group shot down the helicopter and that they were there to clean up loose ends by killing any survivors. The only question in his mind was how to stay alive long enough for the teams to arrive. Given the determination on the men's faces, he didn't believe that was possible.

Although he was wearing a sidearm, Cray realized that, compared to the weapons facing him, he'd have as much chance of surviving as a spitball penetrating a brick wall. Even so, he wasn't going to let anyone detach his and Moretti's heads while they were alive. If he started shooting before they expected it, he'd be able to get off two or three shots in rapid succession before they hopefully shot them. He decided to start with the senior elder since his death would affect the group the most. However, as he reached for his handgun, he felt a gun barrel press firmly against the back of his head, and the firearm wretched from its holster.

"Pashtunwali, pashtunwali," the elder said, repeating this word repeatedly as he approached Cray, who didn't know what he was saying. All he knew was that he was now unarmed, had a gun pressed against his head, and hoped the person holding it had the good sense to pull the trigger and get it over with.

"He's saying you're safe," a person of around eighteen years of age, who was standing at the rear of the group, said in broken English.

"That's hard to believe since you shot down my helicopter and killed everyone but the two of us."

"No Pashtun shot it down. Our honor won't permit it. The governor told us you must have safe passage and not to fire any weapon from sunup to sundown. The elders agreed."

"Someone didn't get the message."

"If we find that person, the elder will deal with him or her harshly."

While they were speaking, the elder directed someone to look at Moretti. After a brief examination, he returned and talked to him. Cray asked the interpreter what he said.

"Your friend has a broken back."

"How does he know?"

The eighteen-year-old passed on the question.

"He says he felt the break and noticed he wet his pants."

"I almost wet my pants when we were shot down."

"I'm a doctor," the man responded in English with a heavy Pashtun accent, making what he said barely understandable. "I've seen this type of injury before. The irregular shape of the spine can only come from a broken back, and losing bladder control usually accompanies such an injury."

Cray didn't want to believe him but knew he was probably right.

"Did you call for help?" the elder asked through the interpreter.

Cray said he did, figuring their knowing that help was on its way couldn't hurt his situation.

Hearing this, the doctor decided not to move Moretti before then for fear of further injuring him. The elder agreed and ordered two men to get a canopy and place it over the captain to shelter him from the sun—the afternoon temperature at this time of year averaging a hundred degrees Fahrenheit. The doctor accompanied them. When they returned, the doctor was carrying two backpacks of medical supplies. Within minutes, he started two large-bore IV lines, giving Moretti resuscitative fluids so his condition wouldn't deteriorate further. As he inserted the last IV, Cray heard a commotion and saw two persons being dragged towards the elder by four rough-looking men. Both had their hands tied behind their backs. One of the four spoke to the elder.

"These men destroyed your helicopter and killed the governor and the five who were with him," the elder said through his interpreter.

"How do you know?"

The elder spoke to one man, who opened the bag he was carrying, showing it was filled with US dollars. Another lifted the metal tube in his hand.

"We found them with the rocket launcher and the money," the interpreter explained.

The elder held out his hand. The gesture was apparent, and someone put a handgun in it. Without saying a word, he put a round into each of the men's heads.

Ninety minutes after Cray called Bagram and told them of Moretti's condition and that the Afghans with them were friendlies, a medevac helicopter landed in Musa Qala. A Chinook accompanied it carrying a special forces squad with an AH-64D Apache Longbow attack helicopter and two F-16 fighters providing cover.

"Thank the elder. We wouldn't be alive if it weren't for him," Cray said to the young interpreter.

"The elder says he regrets the deaths of those with you and the injury to your friend. You only have to ask if you need a favor from him or any Pashtun in the future."

Cray extended his hand, which the elder took. "*Salaam Alaikum,*" Cray said, which meant peace be upon you in Arabic.

"Wa Alaikum Salaam," the elder responded, wishing the same peace would extend to him.

With that, Cray turned and followed Moretti's stretcher onto the medevac.

Watching from the peak of the mountain northwest of the town was a thin man six feet three inches tall, dressed entirely in black and wearing a perahan tunban—the traditional dress for Afghan men which consisted of a tunic shirt, pants, and a turban. To anyone looking at his silhouette in the sun or seeing him from a distance, he looked as Afghan as the person beside him. However, up close, there was no mistaking him as a foreigner— his pale complication and blue eyes betraying him.

"The two men you sent to kill the elders and Cray failed," the thin man said to the Afghan beside him after seeing the elder execute them. "Cray is alive."

"I'll send others."

"He's too well protected in Kabul. I'll deal with him."

"How?"

When the thin man didn't answer, the Afghan moved on. "If he discovers you're the buyer for all the poppy crops in Helmand Province and that you orchestrated what happened, he'll have the US military hunt you down."

"He knows nothing about me or my organization. He only knows that provincial farmers grow poppy plants and sell the sap they extract from the pods. The farmers won't cooperate with any investigation because they don't trust outsiders. The president, government bureaucrats, and local officials won't cooperate with American efforts to destroy these crops because they receive money from me to stay out of it."

"But the president agreed to cooperate with the Americans and persuaded the provincial governor to go along."

"The president and governor are weak-kneed and greedy. They let the Americans talk them into burning every provincial poppy field within the next week, after which they'd appease the farmers by giving them three times what they earn for selling the sap, the payments extending to future generations of their family. In exchange for the farmer's cooperation, the president and governor will receive a king's ransom in gold."

"Cray will start an investigation when he returns to Kabul."

"He won't get anywhere."

"Why take a chance? Put a bullet in him."

"I have something else in mind. Forget about Cray and focus on your new job. As the surviving senior provincial official, the president will appoint you the next governor of Helmand Province," the thin man said to Guzar Durani, who was five feet six inches tall and had a generous stomach and dark foreboding eyes. "He'll want you to restart talks with the Americans and push to take the deal that Captain Cray was bringing to your predecessor. You'll need to counter that. What's your plan?" the thin man asked.

Durani thought for a moment before responding. "I'll start a rumor that the president was afraid of losing the farmers' support and ordered the governor killed and the helicopter carrying the American destroyed. In Afghanistan, treachery is a centuries-old way of countering opponents. He'll lose the Americans' trust and regain that of the farmers."

"Since you'll be the provincial governor and won't support his previous plan, what you're proposing means that the president will need you to affirm that rumor. He'll want your help to let the farmers know he's come to his senses, reversed course, and intends for them to keep their generational way of making a living," the thin man said.

"The farmers never wanted their ancestral poppies fields destroyed, even with the crazy amount of money they were guaranteed because history has taught them that occupational forces never stay forever in their country. When they leave, whatever guarantees they made are over. The only reason they accepted the money in exchange for burning their crops is that the president told them, with the governor's support, that he was sending the army to burn their fields no matter what—shoving the deal with the Americans down their throats whether or not they liked it."

"The president has received considerable money from me to keep the military and local police away from the farmers and my distribution warehouses. The Americans must have offered him substantially more to renege on our deal. I'll send one of my men to see him, who'll say I'm instituting a new pay scale for his protection and to check his offshore account."

"And your operations continue unabated."

"This province grows half the world's opium," the thin man said. "My family has worked hard to build the farmer's trust and eliminate competitors that could interfere with our monopoly as the sole buyer of poppy sap in this province. Protect my interests at all costs by getting rid of anyone you think may be a competitor. I require an uninterrupted flow of opium to satisfy my customers' demand for the product. For this service, you'll get Ahmadzai's share. One word of caution: don't get greedy."

Durani said he understood, believing that making millions and living to spend it worked for him.

# ONE

*2005*

C ray was six feet tall, had sandy brown hair and piercing blue eyes, weighed one hundred seventy-five pounds, and had a jogger's physique. He was the first in his family's history to enter the military, becoming a massive disappointment to his parents, whose roots ran deep in Boston society. Like his grandfather, his father was an investment banker for an international firm, and his mother was a homemaker. As the son grew older, the father realized that he had a fascination for numbers and enjoyed the challenge of solving mathematical problems. Anticipating this meant he would follow in his footsteps; he capitalized on this fascination and began teaching him the intricacies of analyzing a company's financial statements and other helpful banking skills.

Proving to be an exceptional student, he was the valedictorian of his high school class. He received scholarship offers from the three universities to which he applied, ultimately selecting Harvard and graduating in three years with degrees in economics and statistical analysis. His father, expecting him to work at the same firm as he and his grandfather, negotiated the young graduate a six-figure contract with generous perks without telling him. That night, when his father told him, they had a come-to-Jesus moment.

"We didn't discuss that you'd negotiate my employment agreement. I said I was considering working at your firm, but now I want another career option," the young Cray said.

"It's done. You have the office next to mine and start Monday. You can get married and start a family earlier than your peers with your salary and bonuses."

"I know you're looking out for me, but I want a career that will protect this country and our way of life."

"Like being an attorney or senator? There's a lot of money in both professions, and I know someone who could help."

"I want to enter the military."

The father shook his head, not believing what he'd heard. "That's beneath you and would make your mother and me laughing stocks in our social circle. The military is for those who are expendable and won't be missed in life because they don't have other skills."

"We sleep safely in our beds because rough men stand ready in the night to visit violence on those who would do us harm."

"Did you just make that up?"

"George Orwell did. I want to be one of those men who protect our way of life."

"Who put this nonsense in your head?"

"No one. I've thought about this for some time, did my research, and visited an Army recruiting office several times to speak with the enlistment officer and others who served. Pending my enlistment, I've been accepted to the Army's Officer Candidate School. I'll be sworn in tomorrow, if you and mother want to attend."

"If you join the military, your mother and I will be shunned by many of our friends, and I'll look like a fool to those in my office because I couldn't convince my son to take a pile of cash and be financially set for the rest of his life."

"I've never felt so sure about anything."

"There's the door; leave the house key on the table before you leave."

After receiving his commission as a second lieutenant in 2005, Cray was assigned to Fort Benning, Georgia, the regimental headquarters for military intelligence and Army Rangers. He honed his skills for the next two years, learning from the best until he became a warrior. Wanting to see how far he could push himself, and with the encouragement of his commanding officer, he applied for and was accepted to Ranger school, completing the rigorous sixty-one-day course, which had an attrition rate of sixty percent. Upon graduation, he was placed in the queue for reassignment.

The Army Personnel office sometimes doesn't make the most intelligent decisions on what assignments are best suited to a person's skills, often accused of trying to place a square peg in a round hole. However, when whoever was issuing assignments that day saw that Cray graduated from Harvard with degrees in economics and statistical analysis, they decided to continue the young officer's education and sent him to Army intelligence school. When he graduated eighty-three days later, he received orders to be on a plane that would leave in sixteen hours for Kabul, Afghanistan, where he was to be the Ranger's regimental intelligence officer.

*April 14, 2009—Wiesbaden, Germany*

After thirteen months in Kabul, Captain Douglas Cray felt he was on vacation as he left the bachelor officers' quarters at Wiesbaden Army Airfield, Germany, and walked to his office. The base was the headquarters for the 66$^{th}$ Military Intelligence Brigade, a part of the US Army's Intelligence and Security Command, or INSCOM. In a beautiful area in the Rhine's wine region, every day felt like a breath of fresh air compared to Afghanistan—where he was always on the alert for an IED, sniper, or fanatic who wanted to kill an infidel.

Intelligence officers read through a morass of collected data, piecing together snippets of information to get what they're after. Frequently, they extrapolate this information to give commanders the situation they'll face or details relevant to their mission. Cray equated it to assembling a thousand-piece puzzle without knowing what the picture was beforehand. In Afghanistan, he built a solid reputation for his intuitiveness and the accuracy of his reports, which sometimes included the political motivations of their adversaries and how US policies and their allies affected these decisions. Cray's commander took notice of this and summoned him to his office.

"Another one of our allies is packing their bags in Afghanistan and leaving the country," the colonel said to Cray, who was sitting in one of the two chairs in front of his desk. "The latest CIA intel report didn't give an inkling of this, but a certain captain in my command predicted it."

"The CIA probably knew about it and didn't tell anyone," Cray replied.

"Why?"

When he hesitated, the colonel told him their conversation was between them and to speak his mind. He did.

"Their director is a political appointee with little intelligence experience. An appointee will not say anything if it conflicts with the administration's narrative. Also, those below the director may not be telling him everything because they know he's only there as long as the administration is in power."

"How did you know one of our allies was leaving?"

"The data's there. If you look at the media feeds from the other nations who are in-country, you get a sense of their political attitudes. In this situation, if the prime minister didn't pull his troops, he might have been thrown out of office. Their withdrawal was inevitable."

"What about our government?"

"It's a complicated interaction of various interests, at the appointee level and below, inter and intra-agency rivalries, and political interactions."

The colonel looked him in the eye for a few seconds before speaking. "I want you to explain this in detail. I can better organize and focus our intelligence efforts if I understand the dynamics. Put it in writing and be specific so I can pass it on to command because I'm not the only one surprised by this ally's departure. Think outside the box. I want to know if there's a tail wagging the dog."

Although Cray didn't know it, what he was about to write would have profound future consequences, changing his life in ways he couldn't have imagined.

The report took three months to assemble, the data coming primarily from the massive INSCOM database, which connected to a portion of the NSA's data library, both organizations functionally under the Department of Defense. As the colonel requested, he'd documented the tails wagging the dog. One was embedded career bureaucrats, sometimes called the Deep State, who controlled the day-to-day functions of the eighteen organizations comprising the intelligence community. The appointed heads of these organizations would only be in their positions a relatively short time, and they couldn't come close to knowing the thousands of functions and sub-functions over which they held responsibility.

He documented with a series of examples that most of the Deep State influence came from the office of the executive assistant director for intelligence for the FBI, the director of the military intelligence staff for the Defense Intelligence Agency, the deputy director of the National Clandestine Service arm of the CIA, and the Undersecretary for Policy for the Department of Transportation. He showed how these embedded officials manipulated appointees by selectively giving them information and data. After providing additional documentation of their influence on policy decisions, he referenced Bill Clinton, who said: *Being president is like being the groundskeeper in a cemetery—there are a lot of people under you, but none of them are listening.* Not holding anything back, Cray showed how, in some situations, the data that appointees received was inaccurate and in stark contrast to that in other organizational databases, the error resulting in adverse policy decisions.

Cray took the colonel's advice to think outside the box and expanded the scope of his report, taking into account the influence exerted on government policies by social and traditional media organizations. He documented that those controlling these companies shaped public opinion through censorship, the allowance or denial of a post, and banning those who didn't comply with their narrative. He wrote that over time, social media organizations became so ingrained in everyday usage that it would be difficult for all but an authoritarian government to alter its business conduct. Therefore, it was another tail wagging the dog. He named Peter Kimmel, the founder, chairman, and CEO of one of the world's largest social media sites, as the primary gatekeeper for social media platforms, whose influence extended to traditional media.

The last dynamic he addressed was Washington lobbyists, who influenced government and corporate policies by facilitating corruption. He described how these intermediaries were hired by corporations that could not directly contribute to a political candidate because the law prohibited them. However, they could circumvent this restriction by hiring lobbyists, who would hold fundraisers for politicians that the corporation wanted to influence, the politician knowing what the corporation wanted. Cray discovered that the return on investment for the corporation averaged a staggering seventy-six thousand percent. For every dollar the average corporation invested in a lobbying firm, they received seven hundred and sixty dollars in return. Again, he named names and provided examples of their influence.

He submitted his report to the colonel, who found it compelling enough to send to the two-star in command of INSCOM. Afterward, neither he nor the colonel heard anything more. Neither knew that the two-star thought Cray's insights were brilliant. Believing it to be acutely insightful, and particularly concerned with the tail wagging the dog aspect, he sent it to a senior political appointee in the DOD. What he didn't know was that it never reached him. Instead, it was read by a Deep State bureaucrat whose job was to prioritize the appointee's mail. As he read what the two-star sent, a wave of adrenalin coursed through his body, and his heart rate skyrocketed.

By the time he finished the report, he was in panic mode. Because it was unclassified, he could send a copy to the individuals that the report referenced without creating a paper trail. Each received it by the end of the day. However, the bureaucrat knew he was in a catch-22. While he could keep the report out of the hands of the DOD appointee by not giving it to him, he needed to enter its receipt into the system because it was sent by a general officer who might go into his computer and check its status. Therefore, he employed smoke and mirrors to give the appearance that the report wasn't ignored, coding it in the DOD system as being circulated and studied. Because it was one of the thousands of unclassified reports and studies received by the department, he felt it was doubtful anyone would ask to see it. Therefore, the original was shredded, and the pieces were put into a burn bag to be incinerated.

The following day, the bureaucrat, and the Deep State officials mentioned in the report, discussed whether to kill the intelligence officer who wrote it and the general who read and sent it up the chain of command. However, all agreed that an investigation into their deaths would create significant risk because they didn't know whether other copies of the report existed. Therefore, they decided to monitor the author but take no action. Thirteen years later, they reversed that decision.

*July 3, 2012—Fort Belvoir, Virginia*

Major Douglas Cray left Germany five months ago with gold oak leaves on his shoulder and an assignment as a counterintelligence officer to the US Army Intelligence and Security Command, twenty-three miles from the nation's capital. His duties included identifying foreign intelligence threats and developing countermeasures to keep enemy organizations from gathering information. Because the scope of his current position was broader than in Germany, he decided to look at the report he'd submitted to the commander of the 66th Military Intelligence Brigade nearly three years earlier to see if those mentioned in it continued to exercise outsized influence within the government. After two days of data gathering and digging deeper, he discovered that those mentioned had significantly expanded their sphere of influence beyond the United States and were working towards something that, before today, he would have thought was impossible.

This information wasn't easy to assemble because they'd classified whatever they sent and received, placing an SCI, or Sensitive Compartmentalized Information designator on it, meaning only a specified group had access because of the extremely sensitive nature of what was within. Since the NSA could look at anything they wanted, encrypted or classified, Cray could read everything sent and received by the individuals mentioned in his report.

Cray discovered that those mentioned in his report coordinated with a group of like-minded individuals who believed there needed to be a new world order to create global stability. One summary of that belief came in emails between Eugene Gillespie, the director of the military intelligence staff for the Defense Intelligence Agency, and his counterpart in Great Britain. Responding to a question, Gillespie postulated that territorial consolidation didn't require a military component but a lasting merger of populations that resulted when the populace accepted their situation. "They don't have to like the circumstances; they only need to accept this new world order. Global unification will be territorial at first and occur by continent. North America, South America, Asia, and Europe would lead, with Africa and Oceania—Australia and surrounding areas following. Antarctica is inconsequential."

His counterpart agreed, writing that a consolidation of continents would ensue when governments eliminated border security enforcement and provided those who entered their lands with healthcare, education, and other benefits, including limited local voting rights. "As immigrant populations intertwined with those who were indigenous," he wrote, "distinctions between nationalities will fade. Government policies and laws in democratic societies like Great Britain have already changed to reflect this emerging demographic. Eventually, borders will become demarcation lines rather than enforced boundaries and, as continental populations become harmonious and genetically diverse from the offspring of ethnically diverse parents, continental continuity will become the norm."

"Global continuity might take generations longer," Gillespie responded in a subsequent email, "but eventually, the same process that created continental unity will create a new world order."

"Is that what this is about, a new world order?" Cray asked himself. He next looked at the emails from Adam Tanner, the deputy director of the National Clandestine Service arm of the CIA.

"The change won't be immediate," Tanner noted to his counterpart in India. "The merging of cultures and ideas, the election or appointment of those supporting this collectivity, and a cohesive and singular media narrative need time to ingrain."

His counterpart agreed, saying it was like constructing a skyscraper—completing one floor at a time until everyone saw the completed building and accepted it as part of the skyline. "Some will oppose it because it shades buildings," he continued. "Some view skyscrapers as architectural atrocities. Others will oppose the increased traffic or deem it unwarranted because they like the status quo. However, once the buildings are up and there's general agreement by this homogenous society that it didn't significantly affect their quality of life, they'll learn to live with this new world order."

"There it is again, new world order," Cray said. "How are you communicating with one another?" he asked, seeing that the emails he was reading ended years ago. He knew any commercially available cipher was worthless against the NSA's decryption capabilities and would only arouse their interest. Avoiding detection meant avoiding the NSA's data collection network, which he'd been told was an impossibility. Therefore, he wondered, how have they been communicating?

Cray went back to reading the emails, retrieving those from Samuel Bradford, the executive assistant director for intelligence for the FBI; Desmond Pruitt, the Undersecretary for Policy for the Department of Transportation; Peter Kimmel, the founder, chairman, and CEO of one of the world's largest social media sites; and two Washington lobbyists working for different law firms. Each discussed the components of a new world order. Like the others, their emails abruptly stopped some years ago.

It was one in the morning when he finished reading the emails. Pumped by what he'd found, he decided to stay at his desk and keep going. Trying to put himself in their place, he believed that any group orchestrating continental homogeneity needed to meet regularly to remain in sync. Knowing the gathering of such prominent people would raise suspicions unless it was at an established conference or event, he put together a list of possible meeting places, eventually narrowing it down to two—the

World Economic Forum in Davos, or WEF, and the World Social Forum, or WSF, which met at various locations. The WEF was regarded as the more prestigious, with three thousand of the planet's most prominent influencers as participants. The WSF's average attendance was twelve thousand, most of whom were from civil society networks, trade unions, youth and women groups, lobbyists, and academics. Both were annual events.

Digging deeper, he discovered that the WEF espoused the need for economic liberalism, liberal democracy, and a managerial state, in contrast to the WEF, which promoted enhanced regionalism, state-led development, and more robust international regulation of markets. Ultimately, he believed that the World Economic Forum's focus was more aligned with orchestrating a new world order.

He left his office at four that morning—getting a few hours of sleep before cleaning up and changing uniforms before returning at eight and handing his updated report to the commanding general of INSCOM, the same two-star who'd read his first paper. Finding it more compelling than the original, he sent it to the same DOD appointee whose mail was still being prioritized by the bureaucrat. Upon seeing it, that official had an *oh, shit* reaction and forwarded the new report to the same group—one sending it to the thin man.

# TWO

*July 5, 2012—London*

The thin man didn't pick his nickname; it just came to people when they looked at his one hundred thirty pounds, six foot three inches tall frame, which gave him the appearance of being woefully undernourished. The more this descriptive was used, the more ingrained the moniker became in one's lexicon until people used the term "thin man" more than his surname. He was aware of what people called him and took no offense, accepting it as an accurate representation of his appearance. He had multiple residences, although his primary home was in Knightsbridge, the most affluent area of London and the city in which he was born fifty-eight years ago. The average price of a residence in Knightsbridge's "poorer" areas was four million three hundred thousand dollars. He purchased his home cost for an immodest one hundred eighty-three million dollars through one of his offshore trusts.

He walked through London's "the Square Mile," which had the largest concentration of financial companies in the world, unrecognized by anyone. None of the hundreds of sycophants he passed—those who acted obsequiously toward someone important to gain an advantage, knew who he was. If they had an inkling of his wealth or influence, and the size of the offshore fund he controlled, they would have tried to ingratiate themselves to further their business career. However, he wanted to maintain a low profile because he also had an enormous drug distribution business whose funds went into a separate offshore account to be washed before it was sent to the fund his employees saw. Even though his private fund owned numerous profitable companies, each owned by an offshore entity, he didn't want anyone focusing on the math. Therefore, he took great pains to keep his name and that of his fund out of the press and social media. That wasn't difficult since his fund was private, and he was a recluse who didn't enjoy socializing.

To the fund's twenty employees, he was the general manager. He did nothing to stem their curiosity about whose money they were handling, only telling them they were managing the money for a family who shunned publicity. The employees speculated incessantly about who that might be—running the gambit from the Saudis to a Russian oligarch.

The thin man grew up in a military family, living in the West London Borough of Hammersmith. He attended the Royal Military Academy Sandhurst, duplicating the five previous generations of his family who attended a British military academy—entering the army and retiring at forty after twenty years of service. The first generation of his ancestors fought for the British military in Afghanistan to prevent the Russians from going through its mountainous regions and invading India. In command of the garrison at Helmand Province in 1838, his ancestor got to know the farmers in the area he governed and negotiated an agreement to purchase their poppy crops. He sold the sap extracted from it and shipped it as military cargo to London, where chemists converted it to morphine, which was ten times stronger in its pure form than opium. They also produced codeine, which was sold to intermediaries for local distribution since this drug required no prescription.

In the late nineteenth century, a pharmaceutical company buying opium extract to produce codeine and morphine discovered that they could make heroin from the same extract and that it was more effective for respiratory illnesses. However, over the next three decades, they found it was highly addictive when taken intravenously. When the government banned its manufacture and distribution, the family moved the sale of heroin underground. The head of the family didn't care about what happened to those taking drugs. He only cared about the massive profits from selling the opium sap to intermediaries, who took the production and distribution risks.

Over generations, his family continued to work closely with the Afghan farmers, retaining the loyalty of each family head because they'd kept their word and increased payments with rising market prices without being asked. Because of this trust, the tribes continued their exclusive arrangement after the British left Afghanistan and held steadfastly to it.

Although each preceding generation of the thin man's family could have bought the most expensive residences in London, they lived in the middle-class neighborhood of Hammersmith, maintaining a low profile from one generation to the next. Upon retiring from the army, his father broke this cycle by starting a single-investor fund, or fund-of-one, to invest the family money. The law firm he selected had an excellent reputation for establishing this type of legal framework and was known to have clients on both sides of the aisle of respectability. They were particularly eager to get involved because of the enormous amount of money. It went without saying that an immodest amount would stick to their fingers as they used their legal creativity to establish elaborate domestic and offshore strategies to incur additional expenses. Over time, the family's business interests became the dominant part of their legal practice.

When his father died, the thin man, an only child who never married, took over the fund's management, expanding its ownership to twenty-seven companies worldwide. This brought him even more wealth, his business dealings going through cutouts—trusted intermediaries who passed along relevant information and executed his instructions. In most cases, this was his law firm.

When the thin man read Cray's report, he was consternated that an adversary who'd been an irritation to him for the past four years wouldn't go away. He wondered what prompted him to write a follow-on report, this one mentioning for the first time a new world order. How did he come up with that? The good news was that nothing changed from the first report. His contact at the DOD had destroyed both originals after coding their receipt in such a way that they would be next to impossible to find in the index of files. He was most concerned with his mention of Davos, not trusting that Cray wouldn't eventually put together that the individuals he mentioned were part of a cabal and not a loose association of individuals with similar beliefs. In the same position as before about what to do with Cray, the last thing he wanted was to rock the boat by killing him. It was too big a risk to murder the counterintelligence officer because the first thing INSCOM would look at was what he was working on or wrote, after which they'd put a microscope on everything he'd done. When they discovered that the DOD couldn't find a copy of either of his reports, there was no short-circuiting the investigative frenzy that would follow. Therefore, he let Cray live. That decision was a catastrophic mistake.

*January 26, 2021—Davos, Switzerland*

The thin man's residence in Davos, which he used primarily in the winter, cost one hundred eighty-five million dollars, the land a good chunk of that amount. The sixty-thousand square feet mansion had hand-crafted furniture and thirty-five-foot floor-to-ceiling windows, providing a stunning view of the snow-capped mountains they faced. Below the floor at the front of the mansion was a series of rooms that only his security detail, who doubled as his maintenance and cleaning staff, knew existed and were allowed to enter. One of them was his office.

A significant part of the immense cost of constructing his residence was the Faraday cage—a container or shield that prevented electromagnetic radiation from entering or leaving. In practical terms, that meant no one was able to use a cellphone, Wi-Fi, or other electronic devices within the residence because the signal couldn't escape the Faraday barrier, nor could someone outside the house use electronic monitoring equipment to spy on him because it converted his home into a dead zone. In addition to being electronically impermeable, every window had a three-inch-thick layer of bullet-resistant glass.

Although the Faraday cage made it impossible to use the internet or cell phone within the residence, the thin man required a workaround because he ran a multi-billion dollar drug and business empire, which necessitated contact with the outside world. That solution was a shielded cable running from his underground office to a remote satellite dish, giving him unimpeded computer and communications access while in that office. The service tunnel to this dish also served as his escape route, ending at a surface hatch at the edge of the property.

He returned to his residence from the Davos Conference Center after the first day of the World Economic Forum. Most of the three thousand forum invitees from one hundred seventeen countries would spend the evening attending events hosted by corporations, institutions, and governments. The gathering at the thin man's residence, held daily during the forum, didn't issue invitations. Attendance was restricted to the five, ten-member committees that administered the Cabal and the forty-five billionaires whose influence and wealth transcended borders. These ninety-five members, less than a quarter of the four hundred eighty-three who belonged to the organization, were working on the yearly update to the business plan.

Since its inception and founding by the thin man, the Cabal's business plan, which was stringently followed, had a singular goal: to replace nation-states with a borderless global society that had a centralized government over which they'd have control. Achieving this would result in a sanctioned monopoly for every industry because a singular government would determine who received contracts, tax incentives, waivers, and every facet affecting corporate and personal wealth. This executive or dictatorial power, depending on if one looked at the glass as being half full or empty, also meant no term limits, changes in administrations, or political parties with differing opinions. It wouldn't start that way, but that was the transitional endgame.

Success depended on selling the concept of this new world order to those who migrated between borders because the embedded citizenry of whichever country they entered would resist change. That was human nature. The Cabal's public relations teams began with a social and digital media blitz that proclaimed everyone on the planet had the right to live wherever they wanted and also the inalienable right to free education, free medical care, a minimum income, and the right to say how and by whom they were governed—meaning the right to vote. Predictably, these beliefs weren't popular with the ingrained citizenry, who were taxed and had to pay for these benefits, but it was wildly popular with those who lived in other countries and wanted a better life sponsored by the nation into which they migrated.

To encourage and perpetuate this inter-country migration, the Cabal sent organizers to every country from which the migrants came. They gave money, supplies, and medical care to those making the journey and provided food stations and temporary shelters. This type of support was like opening the value on a fire hose, and the number of migrants making these journeys increased exponentially.

The borders of the countries into which these vast numbers of people were going were soon overwhelmed. Without a physical barrier or an adequate number of border agents to patrol the hundreds and sometimes thousands of miles of border, keeping someone from entering a country was equivalent to expecting a sieve to hold water. By definition, that couldn't happen. The migration unfolded, and no one could stop it.

In parallel with encouraging and supporting the migration over borders, the Cabal generously donated to the campaigns of local and national officials who believed in a borderless society and refused to arrest, prosecute, or deport those who illegally crossed their border. Once word got back that there were minimal arrests and deportations, the spigot opened even more.

It began in larger urban cities when politicians realized that the enormous number of new arrivals in their city was an untapped potential voter bloc large enough to elect them to office. Backed by city councils, who had the same underlying interests as the politicians, they fought to allow these non-citizens to vote in local elections, the trend gaining momentum as courts ruled that local jurisdictions could make their own voting rules. The newly arrived migrants quickly became the voter majority in whatever area they settled and cast their vote for those who supported them. As city after city changed their laws, those in government realized they were losing their political base. Within a short time, countries began altering their laws to reflect these new majorities, rapidly moving towards the next transition—a singular society.

To ingrain the normality of a borderless society into future generations, the Cabal contributed hundreds of millions of dollars to school board members' campaigns and the educational institutions' endowment funds that espoused this belief. From kindergarten to university, students were taught this was the new normal. To combat the criticism of parents and anyone else who objected, those who disagreed were suspended or banned from social media and prevented from giving their opinions at school meetings.

The Cabal continued their contributions to politicians who believed in a borderless society. However, the money required to accomplish their objectives continually decreased as politicians caught on that whoever sided with this new voting bloc would be elected to office.

The last phase of the transition to a new world order was the creation of a singular society, which was well underway and the focus of the Cabal's current business plan.

*One week ago—Davos, Switzerland*

The thin man entered his library, which was off the foyer, and pressed a combination into a cipher lock beside a door at the rear before looking into the retinal scanner next to it. When the door clicked open, he descended a broad stairway leading to a long hallway and a suite of rooms. One was his underground office. The thin man sat behind his desk, turned on his computer, and began reading emails. Most were routine business matters. The one from Samuel Bradford wasn't.

The FBI intelligence officer was one of the trusted few to whom the NSA had given access to their undisclosed communications channels. Immediately, he gave his fellow Cabal members the procedures to access and log into the NSA satellites and select these channels.

The reason the NSA established these channels was because of Edward Snowden. The former computer intelligence consultant had leaked sensitive NSA intel to China and Russia, embarrassing the NSA and causing security disclosures of monumental proportions. The NSA responded internally at the highest levels by creating a series of channels for the use of a select few within the United States intelligence community, guaranteeing what was said or transmitted over it would only be known between those communicating and two agency officials. This privacy created a conundrum since the NSA decrypted and recorded all data and voice transmissions that interfaced with satellites, towers, ground, and undersea cables. These intercepts were then routed and stored within their databases.

Therefore, special security procedures were enacted to ensure that what was said or transmitted on these channels remained private. Only the NSA director and Libby Parra, the chief of global issues analysis, were permitted unfettered access. Because restricting access to data was a red flag identifying the information as extremely sensitive, the NSA director instructed a programmer to create an algorithm that directed all NSA databases not to display an index of the data intercepted from these channels. That could only be viewed when keywords from one of two officials were entered into the system. Subsequently, there were no red flags because no one knew the data existed. However, there was one flaw—anyone with the login procedures and a password to these channels could use this communication system. The Cabal had the perfect way of communicating and transmitting data among members.

Bradford's email indicated that Lieutenant Colonel Douglas Cray was attending the World Economic Forum, having found out from Pruitt at the Department of Transportation, who arranged for Cray's flight. Having kept track of him over the years, the thin man knew that he now worked for the president of the United States. This and attending the forum changed his previous view of not harming him.

That he was attending the World Economic Forum meant he'd transitioned from writing reports, which were destroyed before they were read by anyone in the DOD and were therefore of little cause for concern, to acting on the information he'd assembled. His current position posed a danger to the organization because he could bypass Washington's bureaucracy and communicate directly with the president of the United States. If he went to Davos and afterward wrote a report, which was a reasonable assumption, there wasn't a doubt that he'd reference his previous reports in writing or verbally. Once it was discovered that they were sent by the commander of INSCOM to the Department of Defense but were never seen by the appointee to whom they were addressed and couldn't be found, the DNI and DOD would launch investigations. That's when the shit would hit the fan. Because the thin man had extraordinary respect for the tenaciousness of his adversary, Cray needed to die before he set foot in Davos.

Although he'd engaged several killers in the past, the person he'd use to murder Cray was a retired SAS sniper with whom he'd previously contracted. The assassin had no scruples or empathy, didn't ask questions, and was an efficient purveyor of death. More importantly, he wasn't from the United States—which made the subsequent investigation that would follow the lieutenant colonel's murder extensively more difficult.

He negotiated the contract in person in Davos, handing the assassin Cray's photo, information on where he worked and travel habits, future vehicle requests from Pruitt on Cray's two scheduled trips to Dulles and where he would be dropped off, and a fat envelope of euros.

*Two days ago—Herndon, Virginia*

The SAS assassin's name was Theo Richardson. However, those in his military unit and the thin man called him by his nickname, *Striker*, because he had played that position on his school's soccer team before joining the military. He was forty-two years old, bald, five feet four inches tall, weighed one hundred thirty pounds, hazel eyes, and had a smile that brandished crooked yellowed teeth.

Upon his late-afternoon arrival in the United States, he checked into the Hilton Washington Dulles Airport hotel in Herndon, Virginia, three miles from the main terminal. Ordinarily, he didn't like to fulfill a contract at an airport because of the security cameras that usually peppered the facility and surrounding area. However, he didn't have a choice on this hit because this person had no set schedule and only sporadically left his office at the Raven Rock Mountain Complex—a secure military facility.

With those trips made at the last minute, the airport was the only opportunity he would have given the timeline imposed. That meant taking a long shot from one of the adjoining structures, the risk being that he had no control over pedestrians who might walk in front of his target as he took his shot. At a thousand yards, the world needed to stand still for the one point three seconds it took before the bullet impacted.

As Richardson finished his check-in process at the hotel, the front desk clerk saw a note on her computer screen. Telling him to wait, she went into the back room and returned thirty seconds later with a manila envelope. The name on it matched his passport, which was an alias. Opening it in his room, he found keys to a Toyota with directions to where it was parked.

The Toyota SUV was in the second row of the parking lot fifty yards from the hotel entrance. A briefcase in the cargo area contained the tools of his trade. Seeing that no one was around, he opened it and saw the disassembled Vanquish .308 sniper rifle that he requested, which fired rounds traveling two thousand seven hundred and fifty feet per second. Next to it was a Vectronix Vector 23 laser rangefinder, two spare magazines, and a burner phone. He put the phone in his pocket.

Deciding now was a good time to familiarize himself with the airport and find a place to take his shot, he got into the vehicle and followed the signs to the main terminal, where he saw the VIP drop-off point for government vehicles. He continued exploring the airport, looking for an unobtrusive place where he could take his shot. Fifteen minutes later, he found it on the perimeter road where three parking structures, each five stories high, had an unobstructed view of the main terminal.

He entered the first, noting that a waist-level camera photographed the license plate of each vehicle, but there was no camera pointed at the driver's face. Next, he drove to the roof-level parking spots, looking for surveillance cameras along the way. Although he didn't see any, he knew the view from a moving car wasn't always perfect. Parking on the roof, he slowly walked down the ramps until he reached the entrance, seeing no surveillance cameras within the structure. Returning to the roof, he removed the rangefinder from the gun case. He wasn't worried about being seen. With plenty of empty spaces on the four floors below, no one wanted to drive their vehicle to the top, where it would be exposed to the elements and become a target for birds that crossed the structure.

After attaching the scope to his weapon, he walked to the edge of the parking structure and began zeroing it, knowing that it would still be imprecise. Because the weapon had been disassembled and the scope detached, it would be slightly out of alignment, meaning the point of impact would be fractionally off. Usually, he'd take the weapon and fire it at the time of day in which he would take the shot, making micro-adjustments until the alignment was perfect. That meant compensating for barometric pressure, temperature, wind, and light. However, because the thin man told him to avoid unnecessary exposure and not take his weapon into the surrounding countryside for fear he'd be seen, there would be no micro-adjustments. Therefore, he'd need to rely on his two decades of killing people to make the back-of-the-envelope micro-adjustments.

Richardson knelt and looked at the terminal through the Vectronix. Focusing on its exits, he wrote the distances to the doors, the VIP vehicle area, and landmarks in-between. When finished, he had ten reference points, the furthest of which was one thousand thirteen yards away—well within his comfort zone. He wasn't going to miss.

# THREE

Nemesis was an ultra-secret joint United States-China off-the-books non-military organization named after the Greek goddess for retribution against evil deeds. Formed to get around Washingtonian and Beijing bureaucracy, and only known to fourteen people answerable to the presidents of those two countries, its sole purpose was to act quickly to protect both homelands from irreparable harm. Their most recent action prevented two nuclear devices from leveling Shanghai and Beijing, and a dirty bomb from detonating next to the White House.

It was headquartered at Site R, the Raven Rock Mountain complex near Blue Ridge Summit, Pennsylvania, seven miles from Camp David. A secret ninety-seven-and-a-half-mile underground tunnel connected it to the National Security Agency in Fort Meade, Virginia, and the Pentagon in Arlington, Virginia. A branch extended to Camp David—six-and-a-half miles as the crow flies from Site R. Built within caverns, the two hundred sixty-five thousand square feet complex was a series of buildings that served as the Alternate National Military Command Center—the backup facility for the Pentagon. Dubbed initially "Harry's Hole," after President Harry Truman, who ordered the construction of the massive project, its existence has been a poorly kept secret since the day it was built.

The brass plaque outside the entrance to its offices at Site R read: *White House Statistical Analysis Division* and was referred to by those who knew of it as the S-A-D division, pronouncing each letter separately. With the words *White House* in front of its name, the implication was that it was only answerable to the chief executive of the United States. Subsequently, everyone at the complex left them alone and didn't ask what they did.

Although Lieutenant Colonel Doug Cray was the administrative commander of Nemesis, Matt Moretti was its operational leader and ran the show in the field. The thirty-eight-year-old former Army Ranger was six feet three inches tall with a chiseled-cut face and a thick-chested muscular physique. Han Li, who only weeks ago became his wife, was formerly China's top assassin. The thirty-five-year-old Asian beauty was five feet eleven inches tall with an athletic build, porcelain-like skin, long brunette hair, and black opal-colored eyes. She was a head-turner.

Moretti and Han Li were returning from their honeymoon in Athens, Greece, landing at the Washington Dulles International Airport at five in the afternoon. A federal official greeted them at the aircraft door and escorted the couple through the VIP section of customs and immigration and into the baggage claim area, where Cray was waiting.

"You both look rested," he said after shaking Moretti's hand and hugging Han Li.

"How's Jehona?" Han Li asked, referring to their adopted fifteen-year-old daughter, an orphan and former human trafficking victim who was now attending a boarding school in Virginia.

"She became quite the celebrity when the president's helicopter returned her to campus. The school's security is taking her safety very seriously after they were told a Secret Service agent would be shadowing her."

The president told Han Li and Moretti that he'd tell the Secret Service to keep an eye on her so that they could focus on their job and not worry that a wacko would try to get to them through her.

With the couple having only carry-on bags, the three walked outside.

"Thanks for the ride home," Moretti said, "but you also have another reason for being here."

Cray smirked as he shook his head in acknowledgment. "Remind me never to play poker with you. What gave me away?"

"You look as nervous as an EOD rookie about to disarm his first bomb."

"That bad?"

Moretti nodded.

Upon opening the right-side rear door of the black Suburban and letting Moretti and Han Li inside, Cray collapsed to the ground. Because only the sound of the car engine could be heard, Moretti thought he'd tripped. When he saw the blood on his jacket, he realized that Cray had been shot and quickly pulled him into the vehicle. The door was almost shut when they heard the dull thud of bullets bouncing off the vehicle's bulletproof exterior.

"Get to a hospital fast," Moretti yelled to the driver, who switched on the siren and flashers and peeled rubber as they left the terminal area.

"Let's see what we're dealing with," Moretti said as he knelt on the floorboard with his back to the driver's seat. Han Li knelt beside him.

They removed Cray's jacket and shirt to try and find the wound, seeing the impact point of the bullet in his back and blood coming from the hole. Turning him over, they didn't see an exit wound, indicating the bullet was still lodged in his body.

"He's losing a lot of blood. The bullet nicked something," Moretti said as he tore off a piece of Cray's shirt and pressed it tightly against the wound. "Call Bonaquist and tell him to alert the hospital that we're inbound with a gunshot victim who's bleeding out. Every second is going to count because this doesn't look good. He'll need …," Moretti said, grabbing Cray's dog tags, which he always wore, "O positive blood."

Han Li got the name of the hospital the driver was racing to and called Bonaquist. The former Secret Service agent was the number two operative behind Moretti, and Han Li was number three.

On the edge of consciousness, Cray weakly grabbed Moretti's shirt and pulled. Although there was little strength in his grip, Moretti got the message and bent down, putting his left ear near his mouth. "The Cabal," Cray said in a barely audible voice.

"What does that mean?" He never got a response because his face went blank just after he said those words, and his eyes and mouth remained open. Moretti felt his neck for a pulse. There was none, and he began CPR.

"Faster," Han Li told the driver in a voice that said every second mattered.

The driver wove in and out of traffic on his way to StoneSprings, a hospital eight miles west of the airport and twenty minutes away in light traffic. Weaving in and out of traffic with an expertise that would have made the director of *Gone in 60 Seconds* proud, and thanks to the siren and flashers, he made it to the hospital ten minutes after leaving the terminal. Even so, Cray had lost an enormous amount of blood and looked on the fringe of hypovolemic shock, where the body's tissues and organs couldn't get enough oxygen and became damaged. Although the CPR Moretti performed got Cray's heart to beat again, his pulse was almost nonexistent.

Four medical staff were waiting with a gurney at the emergency room entrance and got two IV's going before they rushed the lieutenant colonel inside. While the driver pulled the vehicle forward and out of the way of the entrance, Moretti and Han Li entered the hospital lobby and followed the signs to the waiting room. As they walked, he told her what Cray said.

"The Cabal? I never heard him say that word before."

"I don't know what he was trying to tell me, but I will. When I find out who did this, I will kill everyone involved. Count on it," Moretti said in an angry voice.

"Mind if I help?

Theo Richardson knew he'd made a fantastic shot, given he couldn't definitively zero his scope ahead of time and had to estimate a half dozen variables to solidly put the crosshairs on the target at such a long distance. Cray should have been dead, and he would have been if he didn't turn a hair before the trigger was pulled. Instead of the .308 round hitting him in the heart and killing him instantly, he saw the round hit his back in a location that wouldn't prove fatal. His second or third shot would have proved fatal, but someone pulled the lieutenant colonel into the SUV, and they struck the vehicle instead. Seeing this, he emptied the remainder of his clip into the vehicle in frustration as it sped away.

The assassin returned to his car and left the parking garage, wanting to escape the airport before the authorities established a security perimeter and locked it down. He was already checked out of the hotel and booked on a flight to Great Britain that was due to leave late that evening after the police got what they needed and the airport lockdown ended. However, whether he got on the plane depended on the thin man. It was possible he might want him to stay and see if Cray died from shock or another complication of being struck by the heavy bullet. If he survived, the contract would be unfulfilled, and he might tell him to try again. The next attempt would be substantially more difficult because of the protection the president was likely to provide.

Once he was off the airport property, he pulled into a strip center several miles away and, using the burner phone, called his employer. "The person in question was taken to the hospital, and I don't know their condition," Richardson said without preamble.

"Stay and see if he gets better."

"If he does?"

"Pay him a visit." The line went dead.

Richardson removed the SIM card from the burner, broke it, and twisted the phone apart. The feeling in the pit of his stomach, which was never wrong, told him that completing his contract would get ugly. He didn't know that feeling was an understatement.

*Present day—six p.m. EST*

The United States Secret Service arrived in force at the StoneSprings hospital. After being called by Bonaquist, the president sent them not only to protect the lieutenant colonel in case the sniper or an accomplice wanted to finish the job but also to protect Moretti and Han Li if they were the target and Cray was hit by mistake. The agents set up a security perimeter and cordoned off the lobby so that everyone who entered was searched. Because Cray was shot at the airport and was a federal employee, the FBI became involved and started an investigation. Two agents arrived twenty minutes after the Secret Service to get statements from Moretti, Han Li, and the driver, whom they spoke to first. Since the driver didn't see anything and focused on getting to the hospital quickly, getting a statement and his answer to questions didn't take long. Moretti and Han Li's sessions took substantially more time.

Having coordinated their stories before the FBI's arrival, whose presence Moretti anticipated, they gave a sanitized version of what happened. They omitted what Cray told them, any mention of Nemesis, and what SAD did because, as they explained, their work product was for the president's eyes only and subjected to executive privilege. The FBI agents tried to steamroll them, taking the stance that Moretti and Han Li needed to tell them what Cray did at the White House or face obstruction of justice charges. The two operatives weren't intimidated, and Moretti excused himself and made a phone call. Two minutes after he returned, the agents received an unpleasant call from the FBI director, who said he didn't appreciate receiving a phone call from the president asking why his agents were harassing White House staff and wanting to know information that was subject to executive privilege. Knowing they were on the thin edge of being reassigned to the Nur-Sultan, Kazakhstan, Muscat, Oman, or Islamabad field offices, the agents apologized for any misunderstanding. They said they were good with what they had.

Once the FBI left—Moretti, Han Li, and the two secret service agents assigned to them went to the surgical waiting room on the floor above. Five hours later, a woman in her early forties, wearing green scrubs and looking extremely tired, entered the room. Introducing herself as the surgeon who operated on Cray, she sat on a plastic chair across from them and got right to the point.

"Lieutenant Colonel Cray was struck in the lower right quadrant of his back by a single bullet which nicked one of the lumbar arteries," the surgeon began, explaining there were four pairs of these arteries and that they were branches of the abdominal aorta found on the posterior abdominal wall. "The round that struck him was a high-velocity bullet, which created a pressure wave and secondary cavity in the surrounding tissue."

Moretti said he understood because he'd been shot several times and knew firsthand what happened to the body when a bullet entered.

"We did a computerized tomography or CT scan. Although no organs were hit, the bullet caused tissue damage, and substantial blood loss resulted in TBI or traumatic brain injury."

Moretti and Han Li looked like they'd been slapped in the face.

"Are you telling us he has brain damage?" Moretti asked.

"It's too early to say. The effects of TBI can be temporary—or not," she said after a pause. "The loss of blood flow to the brain means it didn't get enough oxygen. I don't know if that deficiency caused brain damage until the brain has time to try and heal itself. To give it that time, I've put him into a medically induced coma."

"How long will you keep him in that state?" Han Li asked.

"It depends on his brain scans. It could be a couple of days or two weeks. But I won't be the one making that decision. I was told just before I came here that he's being transferred to Walter Reed National Military Medical Center in Bethesda as soon as he's stable. That's a sound decision because they're experts at treating TBI."

Their discussion continued for a few minutes, and once the surgeon left, Moretti took the encrypted cellphone from his pocket and called Vice-President Houck. Both he and the president had earlier texted and asked to be kept up to date on Cray's condition. Moretti didn't find the vice-president's involvement unusual because he was increasingly running point on Nemesis, the president feeling that having them both involved was a more versatile approach. Moretti told him about Cray's TBI and the impending transfer to Walter Reed."

"The president ordered the transfer. I apologize for not telling you beforehand," Houck stated. "He'll get the best medical care in the world at Walter Reed and be easier to protect."

Moretti, who'd been a patient there, agreed.

"There's nothing more you can do for him. Get some rest. The president wants Nemesis to find out who did this and put them out of business. Be at my residence at ten, and we'll discuss how to do that."

Visiting Cray meant that Richardson first needed to find the hospital to which he was taken. Knowing it would be close to Dulles, he did a Google search and saw that StoneSprings Hospital was slightly less than eight miles west of the airport, and Reston Hospital was a little over seven miles east. There was no way of getting into whatever hospital Cray was at to learn if the lieutenant colonel was alive or dead and get close enough to kill him if he survived unless he had the proper creds. Since he worked for the president, he would be under the protection of some government agency.

Before he left Great Britain, the thin man gave him the phone number of a person in DC to contact if he needed anything, saying this was the same person who obtained his vehicle and the sniper rifle. He decided to see if the word "anything" included hospital creds.

After purchasing a couple of burner phones, Richardson phoned his contact. The call went immediately to voice mail.

"I'm new in town and need your help," the assassin said after the beep, giving the number to his burner phone before hanging up. A minute later, his phone rang.

"I'll be in your hotel lobby within the hour," the man, who had an authoritative voice, said before ending the call.

Since Richardson knew that he'd be staying in the US for at least a day or two, he returned to the Hilton and checked into the hotel. Afterward, he sat at a table in the lobby, ordered a pot of Earl Grey tea, and waited for his contact to arrive. He was on his third cup when a five feet nine-inch tall man in his mid-fifties, with neatly combed gray hair parted on the left, and wearing a dark blue Brooks Brothers suit with a white button-down shirt and red tie, sat in the chair beside him. His name was Eugene Gillespie, although he didn't introduce himself.

"Cray will live," Gillespie said in a low voice. His accent was mid-Atlantic—a blend of American and British that gave the impression the speaker was from the upper crust. "But he's under Secret Service protection."

"Where?"

"StoneSprings Hospital. They put him into a medically induced coma because of a traumatic brain injury from extensive blood loss. It's unknown whether he has brain damage. Once he's well enough to travel, he'll be transferred to Walter Reed."

"When will that be?"

"I'm told it'll be within a day or two."

"Then I'll kill him at StoneSprings. Can you get me a hospital ID and a diagram of the hospital with his room? I'll also need a handgun with a silencer."

"Forget a gun or blade. The Secret Service is searching everyone entering the hospital. You'll have to find another way to kill him."

"Understood. When can I have the ID?"

"Your StoneSprings identification badge, a medical license ID card, the diagram you requested, and a set of scrubs will be in the front seat of your vehicle by three tomorrow afternoon. Buy a pair of athletic shoes. Most doctors wear those when they're in scrubs, and you'll look out of place in street shoes. Give me your passport; I'll use that photo for your hospital ID."

Richardson handed it to him. "Can I get these items earlier?"

"Getting what you requested without being traced back to me is an exacting process. Your ID will be authentic, and your name and photo will be in the database as the hospital's resident neurosurgeon. After Cray is killed, it'll be erased."

"Easy-peasy."

"I hate that expression," Gillespie said. "It implies accomplishing something simplistically without the possibility of failure. Have you been listening to what I've been saying? What I'm doing and what you're about to do won't be simple. We both must each perform flawlessly so as not to be discovered."

Richardson remained silent, grinding his teeth and finding it hard not to tell this arrogant prick that he was a professional killer and not the paper jockey bureaucrat he was.

"After Cray is killed, they'll look at the hospital's security footage and run everyone through government facial recognition programs and possibly those of other countries. I can't prevent that. You won't make it out of the country if it's believed that he's been murdered. His death must appear to be a result of his injuries. Even suffocating or strangling leaves telltale indications. I have another option."

Richardson took a deep breath, knowing the prick was right. "What do you suggest?"

"Take this," Gillespie said, handing him what appeared to be a bottle of Visine. "Inside is an extremely potent cutting-edge chemical used by a clandestine organization within the government. It kills without leaving a trace as to how a person died. Put a drop in each of Cray's eyes. It'll instantly be absorbed into the body. Only one drop in each because the more you use, the faster it works. Two additional drops decrease the time to death by a factor of ten. Two drops kill in twenty-four hours, four in two and a half, six in fifteen minutes, and so forth. That's the way I was told the progression works. If a single drop gets on your skin, you'll die in a couple of days. There's no antidote, so wear gloves."

"I'll be careful. One drop in each eye. Twenty-four hours after I visit the lieutenant colonel, I'll be in my favorite pub in London."

"That's the idea. Eventually, the poison converts to chemicals commonly found in the body. That's the genius of the substance you're using. Put the container, rifle, and ID card in the vehicle and park it at the airport when you leave. Place the keys under the driver's floor mat."

"Which parking garage?"

"Anyone except the one from which you took the shot. The car has a tracker, and I'll find it. Anything else?"

"They must pay you a fortune for what you do."

"This is not about money."

Richardson looked confused as Gillespie pushed his chair back to leave.

"Then why are you doing this? I don't understand."

"If you did, you wouldn't be alive."

# FOUR

The vice-president has three offices in the nation's capital. He primarily uses the one in the West Wing because of its proximity to the president. For ceremonial meetings and special occasions, he's photographed at a more ornate one in the Eisenhower Executive Office Building, which is next to the White House. His third office is behind the Senate chamber in the Capitol building. However, when he wants to get away from the prying eyes and ears of Washington, he works from his residence—a nine thousand one hundred fifty square feet, thirty-three room house on the grounds of the US Naval Observatory.

Moretti and Han Li were driven there from their home in Hyattsville, Maryland, which was eleven miles away, by their Secret Service protective detail. Greeted by the vice-president as they entered the foyer, he escorted them to his study, where a steward took Moretti's order for black coffee and Han Li's for green tea. Houck sat on a couch on one side of a rectangular coffee table while his guests were on its twin across from him. Once the steward returned with the beverages and left the room, they got down to business.

"I checked on Lieutenant Colonel Cray this morning," Houck began. "The doctor I spoke with described him as hemodynamically stable, which I learned means his blood pressure and heart rate is almost good enough for him to be transported to Walter Reed. He'll be driven there before noon tomorrow."

Moretti and Han Li said that was good news.

"Here's what we know about the shooting," Houck continued. "The FBI analyzed the trajectory of the bullet that struck him and those that hit the vehicle, extrapolating that they came from a parking structure a thousand yards away. That building doesn't have a surveillance system. Instead, it has waist-level cameras that record the license plate numbers of the vehicles that enter and leave. The Bureau told me they'll assemble a list of the cars that entered and left the structure the day of the shooting, along with the names of their owners." The vice-president took photographs of the parking structure from a folder at the edge of the coffee table and laid them out.

"This attack was well-planned," Moretti said. "The shooter selected that building because it lacked visual surveillance and was line-of-sight to their target. Given the distance involved, we're looking for someone with military sniper training or who lives at a gun range."

"The cameras are visible. I don't think a person who did this level of planning would drive their vehicle inside the parking structure knowing that license plate numbers are being recorded," Han Li said, pointing to one of the photos.

"Nevertheless, the FBI is considering that and the possibility that the bullet which struck him was meant for one of you and hit him by mistake."

"Tell them this professional wasn't after us. They hit their target. It just wasn't a kill shot. He could have nailed Han Li or me anytime between the terminal and the vehicle. We were on either side of Cray and an easy mark. He probably didn't have a clean shot at Cray until we got into the vehicle, and we no longer flanked him."

"Why would someone want him dead?" Houck asked. "He's not an operative, and no one knows who he is or what he does outside of being a White House analyst. That cover ties to his academic background. I can understand why someone might want one or both of you dead. Your faces have been seen in the field, and you've made more than your share of enemies."

"Most of whom are dead," Moretti added.

"The shooter knew he was meeting us at the airport," Han Li added. "If we don't find out how and plug that leak, Cray may never be safe, and everything Nemesis does could be transparent."

"I'll have one of my staff put together a list of everyone who knew that Cray was going to the airport to pick you up."

"There's another problem," Moretti said. "The FBI is investigating the shooting. Since we're looking at the same data, we'll cross paths. When we do, they'll wonder why the president's bean counters are investigating his shooting. We don't want them to take a hard look at us or S-A-D."

"The Bureau has already requested permission to search Cray's office at Site R, hoping to find clues as to who wanted to kill him. The president told the director that couldn't happen until his work product, which is privileged, is secured."

"Won't the FBI director become suspicious about why our statistical analysis is so secret if the president doesn't want to show it to the Bureau? They have top-secret clearances, and some presidents have had them peek under the covers in the past," Moretti said.

"The director is already suspicious after the president told him that Site R is off-limits to his agents, and he won't provide an abbreviated summary of what S-A-D does. That's unavoidable. We don't want the Bureau getting into our computers or paper records at Raven Rock, and we can't hand them analytical reports that don't exist. If they find out we have a joint black ops force with China, the president will be fighting Congress, the alphabet agencies, and the DOD. No one can politically survive those headwinds."

"They'll eventually have to see something," Moretti said.

"Alexson and Connelly need time to segregate and hide the Nemesis database and create a few analytical reports. While the

FBI is prevented from searching Cray's office, your team isn't. See if you can find anything on this cabal."

Moretti and Houck agreed that was a good place to start.

"Is there a discreet way to find out if the NSA or another alphabet agency has picked up chatter or data that mentions a cabal?" Moretti asked. "Cray may not have been the only one looking at them."

"I'll ask the president to call Secretary of Defense Rosen and the DNI. Most of the alphabet agencies are under them." The vice-president stood. "Wait here," he said, "I have something for you." He left the room and returned with their daughter a couple of minutes later. Jehona ran to her stepparents, the reunion emotional.

"I need to take care of some things. I'll be back later," Houck said.

Focusing on their daughter, Moretti and Han Li didn't hear him.

The vice-president returned an hour later to find everyone laughing. "As much as I hate to cut this short, it's time for you to go to Site R," he said.

Moretti and Han Li stood.

"The rest of the team is waiting for you. Take one of the Secret Service SUVs. Their license plates will keep you from getting stopped by civilian or federal law enforcement should you have a heavy foot. When you call it a day, return here and we'll go over what you found."

"It could be late," Han Li said.

Houck brushed off the comment with a slight hand movement.

When Moretti and Han Li left the vice-president's residence, the only thing they knew with certainty was what they wanted to do with those involved in shooting Cray. They had no idea what the word cabal meant other than what they found online in the Merriam-Webster dictionary: the contrived schemes of a group of persons secretly united in a plot. That told them nothing.

As they looked deeper, they discovered there was a cabal for almost anything—from an anti-organic food cabal to one for micronations. Therefore, not knowing what they faced, they were as unprepared as a swimmer believing he was in a wading pool rather than in an ocean seeded with chum and surrounded by sharks. When that analogy eventually played out, the team would find themselves in a situation where they were on their own, unable to summon help, and certain they were returning to Washington in a coffin or buried somewhere they'd never be found.

Moretti and Han Li entered the tunnel to the Raven Rock Mountain Complex at the Pentagon and arrived at their destination in a little over an hour and a half. They presented their White House creds to the guard at the exit gate's security station and watched as he slid them over an optical reader, which verified not only that they had access but displayed on the guard's LED screen the faces embedded in their ID's and those taken by the facial recognition camera that looked through the vehicle's front window. When he saw they matched, he lowered the six bollards that blocked the road. Each was eight inches in diameter, weighed two hundred pounds, and extended forty-eight inches below ground and thirty-six above, capable of stopping a fifteen thousand pound vehicle traveling at fifty mph. They parked the SUV in the lot directly in front of them. The walk to the Nemesis offices took only a few minutes as it was the first door to the right as one entered the massive complex.

Putting his hand on a biometric hand reader, Moretti entered his PIN into the keypad beside a bronze plaque that read *White House Statistical Analysis Division*. After hearing the audible click of the lock releasing, he and Han Li entered and were greeted by operatives Jack Bonaquist, Blaine McGough, and Jian Shen. Kyle Alexson and Mike Connelly, former NSA analysts and uber techies, also left their offices to see them.

Bonaquist, an ex-Secret Service agent who was thirty-five years old, weighed two hundred forty pounds, and was six feet eight inches tall with jet black hair, blue eyes, and a face that reflected the square-jawed sternness of someone who did not mince words. McGough, the former Force Recon Marine standing to his left, was six inches shorter. The twenty-eight-year-old was three hundred five pounds of solid muscle and had dark brown hair and brown eyes. The last operator, Jian Shen, was to Bonaquist's right. The twenty-six-year-old captain in China's PLA was the team's sniper. He stood six feet two inches tall, weighed one hundred sixty pounds, and had short black hair and dark brown eyes that were almost chocolate.

"What happened?" McGough asked, wanting to hear firsthand what occurred.

"Let's go into the conference room, and we'll explain."

Moretti and Han Li led the way. When everyone was seated, he and Han Li went over what happened and their discussion with the vice-president.

"He believed the Cabal, whatever that is, was responsible for the attempt on his life," Bonaquist said. "He may have a file on them."

"Cray comes from an intelligence background where everything is documented, and supposition takes a back seat to the facts," Moretti said. "I can't recall a meeting where he didn't pull out a thick folder giving us data on what we were potentially facing."

Everyone nodded in agreement.

"Did Cray have you gather anything on what he called the Cabal?" Moretti asked the two techies.

Alexson and Connelly shook their heads in the negative.

"Check the Nemesis database and see if he mentioned that word in any of the data he collected or notes he made," Han Li said.

"Good idea," Connelly replied. He and Alexson left the conference room, returning fifteen minutes later saying that the word cabal didn't appear in their database.

"Maybe he kept the file in his safe," Shen suggested, with everyone agreeing it was worth a look.

Because only Cray and Moretti had the combination, Moretti went into his office and opened the four-shelf safe, which was fifty-nine inches high, thirty-six inches wide, and twenty-four inches deep. Inside, he found a stack of one-time pads; five classified documents from several intelligence agencies with *POTUS Eyes Only* stamped in red at the top; passports with aliases for each team member; credit cards in those names; and approximately three hundred thousand dollars in various foreign currencies. Not a scrap of paper contained the word *cabal*. Striking out on the safe, the team searched the rest of his office but found nothing.

"Does he have a safe at his house?" McGough asked.

"He does, but he wouldn't keep anything classified there when he works at one of the most secure facilities on the planet. It would be here. Besides, he was married to his job and routinely worked here late, spending several nights a week in the complex's visiting officer's quarters," Moretti said.

"Was he carrying a flash drive?" Shen asked.

Moretti thought for a moment. "That's a good question. I don't know what he was carrying," he said.

# FIVE

StoneSprings Hospital was a state-of-the-art two hundred and thirty-four thousand square feet acute care and surgical medical facility. The first new hospital constructed in Loudoun Country in the last century, the one hundred twenty-four all private bed facility, with fifteen emergency room bays, resided on a fifty-one-acre patch of land in northern Virginia.

Richardson, who wore black scrubs, and black Oc athletic shoes, had his employee identification card clipped to his pants pocket and entered the hospital lobby at four p.m. A dozen feet inside the door was a rope barrier that prevented anyone from proceeding further without going through security. There were three people in front of him, and when his turn came, he unclipped and handed the Secret Service agent his hospital ID card. Typing the name on his computer terminal, the agent confirmed he was a staff member and that the photo on his screen matched the person standing in front of him. Cleared, Richardson's walked a half dozen paces to the metal detector, where he was told to remove anything metal from his pockets. He placed his vehicle key in a plastic container and walked through the sensor without issue.

He took the elevator to the third floor, having no trouble finding Cray's room because a Secret Service agent was standing outside the door. Deciding he needed a reason to enter his room, he went into the nurse's station halfway down the hall, took one of several stethoscopes off a side table, and draped it over his neck. He then put on a pair of latex gloves, which he pulled from one of several boxes at the station.

As he approached the agent, he unclipped his ID card, handed it to him, and watched as his name was verified on the list of hospital employees. The agent then opened the door and let him pass. Two steps inside, Richardson abruptly stopped when he saw a tall thick-chested man and an attractive Asian woman standing beside Cray's bed.

"I didn't know the patient had company," Richardson said, having gotten rid of his British accent.

"He's a colleague," Moretti responded, intentionally keeping their relationship vague.

"I was about to examine him. While I do, you'll have to wait outside," he said in an authoritative voice. "It will only take a few minutes, after which you can stay as long as you wish."

As Han Li started towards the door, Moretti grabbed her hand and shook his head in a barely perceivable motion that indicated something was wrong.

"We're staying," Moretti said, looking Richardson directly in the eyes.

"Hospital policy doesn't permit visitors to be present when a patient is examined."

"What department do you work in?" Moretti asked, ignoring Richardson's statement.

"I'm a neurosurgeon," he replied, handing over his badge, which had the Department of Neurology printed under his name. Moretti looked at it closely before giving it back.

"We both work for the White House. Think of us as part of his security detail if that makes it easier for you. If it doesn't, that's too bad because we're not leaving."

"I could have you removed by security."

"Not likely. Let's call the hospital administrator and see what he says."

Richardson knew he couldn't let that call happen or raise hell with hospital security or the Secret Service agent outside the door. Even though he was on the employee list because of a sleight of hand by Gillespie, neither the administrator nor anyone in the Department of Neurology would know him. Therefore, he reluctantly agreed to let them stay. After looking at the readings on the bedside monitors, the British assassin took the stethoscope off his neck and pretended to listen to Cray's heart. Afterward, he began removing the tape over his eyelids.

"What are you doing," Moretti asked.

"His eyes are dry because he can't blink. I'm going to put some drops on them," Richardson responded, not knowing if that was true, but it sounded reasonable.

"That's curious," Han Li interjected, "because the physician who left seconds before you arrived put antimicrobial ointment in them and told the nurse with her not to remove the tape. That should be on his chart. You might want to look at it."

"These drops won't conflict with the ointment."

"Visine?" Moretti said, looking at the bottle in Richardson's hand and shaking his head. The hard stare he showed the former SAS operative showed he didn't believe a word of what he said. "Maybe we speak with the physician who just left. You must know her."

"This is ridiculous. I'm the only doctor in this room, and I decide what's best for a patient," Richardson said, stripping off the surgical tape over Cray's right eye with his left hand and then removing the plastic cap from the Visine bottle.

Because Moretti was on the opposite side of Cray's bed, he was too far away to do anything but watch the assassin pull back Cray's right eyelid and move the Visine bottle towards it. But Han Li was beside Richardson, and with a hand speed of forty-five mph, the martial arts expert grabbed his hand in a vice-like grip so tight the SAS sniper squeezed the bottle of Visine and sent a stream of liquid onto his face and into his eyes. Because of the bottle's direction, none of it touched Han Li.

Richardson screamed, dropped the bottle on the floor, ran to the sink, and began vigorously washing his face and hands with liquid soap. Short of breath and gasping for breath like a guppy out of the water, he vomited into the sink and, disoriented, stumbled towards the door. Two steps later, he dropped to his knees, stopped breathing, and fell on his left side.

"Whatever was in that bottle was extremely potent," Moretti said. "I wouldn't be surprised if he was the shooter and came back to finish the job."

"Let me get a photo of his face and his prints."

Moretti removed his cell phone from his pocket and took several pictures of Richardson's face, after which he put on a pair of latex gloves from a box next to Cray's bed. He removed the plastic impact cover from the back of his cellphone and, after washing it with soap and water and drying it off, pressed Richardson's fingers to it, put the cover in a vomit bag, and slipped it into his jacket pocket. Searching the body, he found a British passport, vehicle key, physician and hospital identifications, wallet, and a small amount of cash. He placed everything but the passport and two identifications into one of the plastic bags stacked on a bedside table. He was exceedingly cautious when handling the bottle of Visine, placing it in a latex glove and tying the end before putting it in a separate bag.

"Let's see who he is," Moretti said after changing gloves. "The name on the ID cards and passport don't match."

"I'll go with a forty-two-year-old Brit named Theo Richardson," Han Li said, holding up the passport.

"I think you're right. How did this person get these IDs and have his name inserted into the hospital computer system within a day? You and I know that was inside the Visine bottle was so sophisticated that it was only something a government could give to an assassin."

"Which also explains the identifications and computer security verifications."

"This sounds like an attempted assassination from a nation-state," Moretti said. "The FBI would come to the same conclusion. I don't think we should hand over the Visine bottle and what we took off the body to the Bureau or the local police."

"Because they'll take a harder look at Cray and S-A-D. They'll also wonder how two bean counters, even one who was an ex-Ranger, became suspicious about the bottle of Visine and overpowered an assassin," Han Li said, knowing where Moretti was going.

"That's what I'm thinking."

"What now?"

"We tell the Secret Service agent outside the door what happened. I'm surprised he didn't hear the commotion and rush in," Moretti said.

"These rooms must be soundproof because I can't hear anything outside." Han Li opened the door to see if she was correct, and a flood of noise entered the room. The agent turned around and saw the body on the floor.

"What happened to the doc?" he asked, rushing into the room.

"Don't touch the body," Moretti cautioned. "He may have contracted a disease."

The agent backed away as if Richardson had the plague and said something into his mic that neither Moretti nor Han Li could hear.

"We should leave," Moretti whispered. "It's going to get crowded in this room, and I don't feel like answering questions for the rest of the day. I particularly don't want to be frisked."

"You two need to stay until my supervisor arrives," the agent said, seeing them going towards the door.

"We need to brief the president," Moretti replied. The agent didn't have a comeback for that statement and let them pass.

"Let's go to the parking lot. I want to check something out before this place gets thick with law enforcement,"

Moretti said once they were in the hall. As they walked to the elevator, he called Vice-President Houck and told him what had happened.

"I'll back up your story that you needed to brief the president about what happened, but we can't prevent the FBI from questioning you without arousing suspicion."

"We know. Because we left before they could question us about the body, the Bureau and local law enforcement will consider Han Li and me to be persons of interest."

"That's because you legitimately are. Where are you going now?"

"To search Richardson's car before the Bureau impounds it."

"Keep me informed."

"What did he say?" Han Li asked.

Moretti told her.

Parking at StoneSprings hospital was free, with the garage located beneath the hospital. Because of the logo on the key fob, they knew they were looking for a Chevrolet. That narrowed it down, although Chevy's were around fifteen percent of the vehicle market. Looking at the fob, Moretti had a thought and touched the alarm indicator. The horn sounded, and the lights flashed on a black Chevy Tahoe with government plates. It was ten feet in front of them.

"This gets more interesting by the minute," Han Li said, looking at the plates.

They searched the vehicle, finding the briefcase with a disassembled Nemesis Arms Vanquish .308 sniper rifle in the cargo area.

"I'm betting the bullet they took out of Cray came from this rifle," Moretti said.

"Leave it for the FBI or take it with us?"

"The Bureau doesn't have a good track record for sharing work product. We've taken everything else; we might as well take the briefcase and see what we can find. At least we've made it easy

47

for them to find Richardson's vehicle," Moretti said, pointing to a security camera.

"What will you tell the FBI when we meet?"

"As little as possible. For all we know, whoever did this might have a contact in the Bureau."

"They won't like that we've removed something from the vehicle and are withholding information," Han Li said.

"It'll get ugly. They'll threaten us with obstruction of justice and any other charges their creative minds can conjure and put a 24/7 tail on us."

After Moretti took a photo of the Tahoe and its government license plate, he held up the fob to the surveillance camera and put it on top of the driver's seat visor. As they walked to their car, Moretti received a call. It was Vice-President Houck.

"The president got a call from the FBI director saying that, given what happened, they're moving Cray to Walter Reed.

"When?"

"As we speak. I'm told he's on his way down."

Having no idea where such a transfer would occur, Moretti asked the first employee he saw and was told that the emergency room entrance was also the exit for anyone departing the hospital by ambulance. She pointed them in the right direction.

They got more than a few looks as they ran through the emergency room corridor, past that reception desk, and went outside. In front of them, Cray was on a gurney with two chest straps securing him to it and two IV bags dripping fluids into his arms. He was about to be put into an ambulance with three men in suits watching from beside the government vehicle behind it.

Moretti ran to the ambulance, one of the two Secret Service agents beside Cray, who had been the person outside his hospital room, telling the other agent it was alright. The ex-Ranger bent down and whispered in Cray's ear. Once he finished, the gurney was pushed inside, and the ambulance doors closed. The vehicle sped away with its sirens blaring and the government car following.

"What did you say to him?" Han Li asked.

"Later. We came to the hospital to search Cray's belonging for what he had on him the night he was shot."

"And we didn't do that," Han Li confirmed."

"I didn't see any plastic bags or boxes on the gurney. I think the Bureau was so rushed to get him to Walter Reed that they didn't think about his belongings. They're probably still in his room. We need to look through it before the FBI comes to the same conclusion as us."

They rushed to Cray's room and found the door closed, but no police seal was across it, not that it would have mattered.

Richardson was on the floor with a sheet over him.

"I'm surprised the police and medical examiner aren't here," Han Li said.

"It won't be long. Getting Cray to Walter Reed was the Bureau's priority," Moretti said as he opened the narrow clothes cabinet to the left of the bed. "Got it."

Han Li, who was looking in the drawers on the opposite side of the room, came over and saw he was holding two plastic bags.

"Let go someplace quiet," Moretti said, leading the way into the hall. Remembering the empty room they passed near the elevator, they went into it and closed the door.

The first bag contained only clothing. The second had two personal items—dog tags and a wallet with cash, credit cards, a military Common Access Card, or CAC, and his White House ID.

The CAC was a "smart" card issued to active duty military and selected reserve, civilian employees, and eligible contractors. It enabled them to access specific buildings, controlled spaces, and areas of the DOD network. Han Li looked closely at the wallet, hoping to find a secret compartment or re-stitched section. There were none. While she was doing this, Moretti picked up the dog tags. Prior to 2007, these were imprinted with the person's name, blood type, religious preference, and social security number. Subsequent tags replaced the social security number with a randomly generated ten-digit Department of Defense identification number.

"The only other dog tags I've seen are yours," Han Li said, looking over Moretti's shoulder. "What's this?" she asked, pointing to a piece of felt affixed to one of the tags.

"It keeps the two metal tags from clinking. I have an elastic strip around mine, and I like it because it's thinner than felt."

Moretti set the tags down next to Cray's CAC, which he was about to return to the wallet when his eyes locked on a discrepancy. "Look at this," he said, holding the CAC next to the dog tags.

Han Li saw it immediately. "The numbers on the dog tags and CAC don't match."

"They should because a person only has one DOD ID number. Let's see what Connelly and Alexson can find out," Moretti said, throwing everything back into the plastic bags.

As they left the room, they saw two police officers speaking to someone at the nurses' station, who pointed in their direction. Trying not to appear anxious, they continued down the hall, passing the officers on their way to the elevator. When the doors opened, several FBI agents got off.

"Timing is everything," Moretti said as they entered, and he pressed the button for parking.

"Is now a good time for you to tell me what you said to Cray?"

"I reminded him of something that hopefully his subconscious will absorb."

"Which is?"

"*You're a warrior, and warriors don't give up; they don't back down. Pick up your sword, your shield, and fight.* It's a Ranger saying."

"Meaning he should fight to stay alive, his survival giving the person who attacked him the middle finger," Han Li said.

"That's one interpretation."

"And the other?"

"Wake up and help me kill whoever did this to you."

"I like your interpretation better."

# SIX

Adam Tanner was the deputy director of the National Clandestine Service arm of the CIA. The forty-four-year-old was a career bureaucrat who worked at the Agency for twenty-one years and was a Deep State swamp creature, meaning a non-elected influential government official who parceled out true and false information to influence those voted into office. He was six feet three inches tall and white as a sheet because he rarely went outside other than to get to his vehicle. The bureaucrat was neither athletic nor flabby, had salt and pepper hair combed straight back, and wore antique brown Oliver Peoples Coleridge glasses. His office attire never varied, consisting of a dark blue suit, white button-down shirt, some type of striped tie, and highly polished black Beckett Simonson wingtip shoes. Another swamp creature, Eugene Gillespie, sat in a chair in front of his desk.

"Instead of taking care of the problem, Richardson put us in damage control mode," Tanner told Gillespie.

"More accurately, crisis management," Gillespie corrected. "The Secret Service has a record of Matt Moretti and Han Li, the two who were with Cray the night he was shot, being in his hospital room when Richardson arrived. Since there was no identification on his body, nor the Visine bottle, I assume they have it. The Bureau has a surveillance video of them taking

Richardson's briefcase, which contained the sniper rifle, from his vehicle."

"If anyone in the Agency's senior management knows a bottle of Visine was near the body, or Moretti and Han Li ask them about it, they'll know the cardiac inhibitor came from me since I was the only person in the last three months to access the safe in which it was stored."

"We'll get Richardson's items back, including the bottle, so that you can return it to the safe."

"Cray would have been dead had I been allowed to get rid of him with local talent, as I suggested," Tanner vented. "The thin man shouldn't have overruled me and given the contract to an outsider. I would have hired a local to take care of Moretti and Han Li."

"You realize killing two people who work for the White House will draw great attention? The thin man won't like it, especially since we're close to achieving our goals."

"What do you suggest?"

"We frame them. It's clean and will have the White House playing defense. We'll use the hospital surveillance video that shows them taking a briefcase from the rear of Richardson's vehicle and putting it in their car."

"The briefcase alone doesn't mean much unless we get it back with the rifle in it. Otherwise, it's just a briefcase. However, there's no doubt they killed Richardson since Cray was in a coma," Tanner said.

"The briefcase shows an association with Richardson. Otherwise, why did they take it?"

"Good point. How do we get around Richardson impersonating a doctor?" Tanner asked.

"We don't. He was part of the plot. They gave him the sniper rifle and killed him in Cray's room so that he'd be the fall guy."

"Then why take the briefcase from the vehicle?"

"We're creating a narrative to fit the situation," a frustrated Gillespie said. "We work with the hand we're dealt. What's in the briefcase isn't as important as showing an association between parties."

"Which means they hired Richardson."

"That's the narrative. Meeting Cray at the airport was meant to deflect attention from them. When the attempt on his life failed, they switched their focus to killing him at the hospital. That's the story I'll give Bradford, which will be enough for him to issue arrest warrants for Moretti and Han Li for Richardson's murder and an attempt on Cray's life."

"What plausible reason would we give for them wanting to kill Cray?" Tanner asked.

"I thought about that. Because Moretti's wife is Chinese, we'll say they're Chinese spies, and Cray discovered what they were doing and was going to report them. They found out and decided to kill him."

"I like it. They'll be guilty until proven innocent. It'd be political suicide for the president to interfere or come to their defense while this is playing out," Tanner stated.

"The accusations of spying will automatically make them flight risks, and they'll be denied bail. It'll be easy to have them killed in prison. The thin man will go along and let you hire a local to kill Cray before he recovers and reemerges as a threat," Gillespie stated.

"You'll call him?"

"I'll ask him face-to-face in Davos. We'll be there tomorrow."

"Better. When we get the thin man's approval, I'll call Bradford. It shouldn't take him long to get the arrest warrants. I'll suggest Moretti and Han Li be taken to the federal detention facility on D street, where several guards have done favors for me in the past."

That statement brought a nod and a smile from Tanner. "Problem solved," he said.

However, what happened next resulted from the law of unintended consequences making matters much worse.

The FBI employs thirty-five thousand people—fourteen thousand agents and twenty-one thousand professional staff. Its Washington, DC headquarters is a two million eight hundred thousand square feet building, three stories of which are below ground. The Bureau has fifty-six domestic field offices, three hundred fifty satellite locations, and sixty legal attaché offices in US embassies.

Samuel Bradford was a blue blood. Even though his position as the executive assistant director for intelligence garnered respect within Washington society, so did many other government positions. However, none of those occupying these positions had ancestors who arrived on the Mayflower at Cape Cod in sixteen twenty, which was essential if one viewed their blood as blue instead of the red coursing through the veins of commoners. The blue blood was five feet nine inches in height, slender but not thin, clean-shaven, with black hair styled a conservative taper cut. Vain about his appearance, his teeth were regularly whitened, and his body spray tanned every ten days at his plastic surgeon's office— the physician having tightened his neck, arms, and anything else that sagged. He graduated from Yale and was a member of the secret Skull and Bones society, just like Tanner and Gillespie, and used his contacts with others in the society to further his career.

Gillespie discussed his plan with Bradford, a fellow member of the Cabal, prior to leaving for Davos. The FBI intel officer wasn't attending, conflicted by a Senate intelligence committee meeting where he was called to testify. He'd asked Gillespie to brief him when he returned.

"It's obvious that Cray, Moretti, and Han Li need to die," Bradford stated as if it was a routine business decision. "I'll get the information I need for their warrants from the government database and have them arrested by the end of the day."

"Will the director authorize issuing the warrants for members of the White House?"

"He will after I explain the situation to him."

Gillespie said that he was impressed with Bradford's power,

stroking the blue-blooded narcissist's ego. He'd done this in the past, making their discussions go smoothly.

"Where are they now?" Bradford asked.

"I don't know."

"How do you know they'll be in or around Washington?"

"I don't. They work for the White House. Where else would they go?"

"It doesn't matter. Once the warrants are issued, I'll ask the US Marshall to find and arrest them—wherever they are."

"They need to be held incommunicado to maintain the narrative."

"I can't prevent the president from speaking to them. Technically, everyone in the government works for him. How fast can they be suicided?"

"The same day they're put in a cell."

When Moretti and Han Li returned to Site R, they gave Alexson and Connelly Cray's CAC and dog tags, asking them to figure out why there was a discrepancy in the numbers. It took them less than a minute to determine that the Department of Defense ID number on the CAC was accurate and that the one on the dog tags didn't correspond with any identification number in a government database.

"Do you have any idea what that number means?" Han Li asked.

They confessed they didn't but would get working on it. An hour later, they returned to the conference room and told the team that the numbers on Cray's dog tags were a cipher for an email address.

"For those of us not in the Matrix, what does that mean?" Blaine McGough asked.

That comment brought a chuckle from Alexson, a big fan of Keanu Reeves movies. "Each number corresponds to a letter in the alphabet. For example, one may equate to the letter A. In this cipher, it equates to K, two equates to L, and so forth. The sequence of numbers on the dog tags gave us a password-protected email address."

"And you got past the password protection," Moretti said, seeing the lack of tension in the tech's faces.

Connelly confirmed they did. "Cray sent hundreds of emails to himself, the first as far back as 2007," he said. "That was a clever way to hide information in plain sight as long as you know the email address and password."

"I'm guessing Cray knew if anything happened to him that one of us would discover the discrepancy in ID numbers, and you and Alexson would be able to break the cipher and hack the internet provider," Moretti stated.

Everyone went along with that assumption.

"I'll break the emails into groups, so this will go faster. When we finish, we'll give a summary of what we read and focus on the emails we feel are the most important."

It was slow going, not only because of the number of emails but because many contained attachments. Reading through the night without a break and munching on the pizza the techs brought from the cafeteria, they finished at four in the morning, each person printing the emails and attachments they wanted to discuss.

Bonaquist was the first to summarize what he read, saying there's a significant amount of data. However, without names it was difficult to determine if one group was behind the massive inter-country migration the world was experiencing or if the concept caught on, and many others adopted this way of thinking.

"That was my conclusion until I read the reports that Cray wrote in 2009 and 2012," Moretti said. He handed copies to the group.

"Why aren't these in any of the databases we checked?" Moretti asked Alexson, who was in the conference room with Connelly.

"They should be because Cray's emails show they were sent from the commander of INSCOM to the DOD, and there's a record of their receipt and a notice of distribution for review, but the reports are not in the Department of Defense database. They've been deleted."

"That's not surprising given the positions in the government of those named in the report," McGough responded.

"That's the bad news. The good is that we have the reports, know the names of the government officials involved, and can start our investigation with them," Moretti said.

"How can they keep a clique of this magnitude under the radar of global intelligence services?" Shen asked.

"We're going to find out. We know these people are involved with the attempts on Cray's life," Moretti said, holding up the reports. "What I don't understand is why. He wrote the reports in 2009 and 2012. Why wait a decade to try and kill him if he was a threat?"

"When they deleted the reports and emails, he was no longer a threat. Then something happened to change that," Han Li said.

"Now we have to find what happened," Bonaquist said.

"I have an idea," Han Li said, "holding up one of the papers in her hand. "This is the last email he sent himself, discussing the possibility that the Cabal meets in a public venue to avoid such a large gathering standing out. He suspected that was in Davos, Switzerland, at the annual World Economic Forum or WEF—a recognized venue for international influencers where their meetings would go unnoticed."

"If the other members in the Cabal are as prominent as those in the reports, there aren't many venues where their attendance would go unnoticed. The World Economic Forum would be at the top of that list," Bonaquist concurred.

"It's the perfect cover," Moretti agreed.

"When's the next meeting in Davos?"

"Next week," Han Li answered after looking up the date on her cellphone. "It's an invite-only event that brings together around three thousand political, business, and other influencers to discuss global issues and possible solutions to these problems," she continued, reading from a summary.

"We need to attend," Moretti stated.

"If we can get an invite," Shen countered.

"All it takes is a boatload of money," Han Li replied after expanding her Google search. "An annual membership to the forum, required if you want to purchase a ticket, is fifty-two thousand dollars. Add to that the cost of the ticket, which is nineteen thousand. If you want to go to the private industry sessions, that cost is one hundred thirty-seven thousand dollars. All this assumes someone goes by themselves. If they bring a colleague, you jump to another category and pay the industry partner fee of two hundred sixty-three thousand dollars plus the cost of two tickets, bringing the price to three hundred one thousand dollars. If the five of us went, we'd be in the strategic partner category. With the price of the tickets, the cost would be six hundred twenty-two thousand dollars plus travel and lodging."

"Those prices will keep out the riff-raff,' McGough said. "How long does the conference last?"

"Four days."

"If the president approves the funds, we'll attend as the White House Statistical Analysis Division, which will give us access to anyone in Davos who wants to get a message to the president and influence his decisions. That's almost every person there."

"We have the names of a few members of the Cabal, but we don't know its leader or other members who will be in Davos. That means we have a suspect list of three thousand names," Shen said.

"It also requires a change from using blunt force trauma to becoming investigators and using tact and diplomacy to accomplish our objective," Bonaquist replied.

"Let's go back to the attacks on Cray," Han Li said. "Our internal security protocols are airtight. How did someone know he'd be at the airport to pick us up? We didn't even know."

"The only explanation is a government mole who provided the shooter with this information," Moretti answered. "We might want to start with Desmond Pruitt, the Undersecretary for Policy for the Department of Transportation. If we look deep enough, I think we'll find that government vehicles are part of his domain."

"That seems reasonable," Bonaquist said, with everyone else agreeing.

"Jack, look at that while Han Li and I speak with the president about the funding for Davos. I'll have Alexson and Connelly run the photos and fingerprints we took on the Brit who tried to kill Cray and see what they find. I'll also have them assemble a list of those who attended the forum for the past ten years. Going with Cray's assumption that they've been meeting there for at least that long, the rest of the team will look at the individuals on that list."

Once everyone knew what needed to be done, Moretti and Han Li drove back to Washington.

Moretti phoned President Ballinger on their way to the White House. Cleared to park inside the gates, an area reserved for senior staff, they pulled into the space beside two Secret Service officers who escorted them into the building. They showed their creds, just as they did to the guard at the entry gate, and passed through a magnetometer. Once patted down, the agents escorted them to the Oval Office.

The president came from behind his desk and warmly greeted them, directing them to sit on the couch across from his. In preparation for their arrival, a pot of green tea for Han Li and pots of coffee for Moretti and the president were on the coffee table between them. After the steward filled everyone's cups, he left the room with the two Secret Service agents.

Moretti explained what happened at StoneSprings, the discovery of Cray's cipher and emails, his reports, and their belief that the Davos forum was the meeting place for the secretive group called the Cabal.

"I'd like to throw those government officials in jail tonight," the president angrily stated. "But, from what you said, the proof of their involvement has been erased from the government's databases."

"There may be a way to get the information we need to bring down the Cabal, including these individuals."

"You've got my attention."

"We want to go to the Davos forum, sir, but the cost is steep."

"How steep?"

Han Li gave the number.

"It's a better use of taxpayer money than some of the bills Congress sends me. I don't want to leave any stone unturned. If you feel attending the World Economic Forum is important to uncovering those in the Cabal, I'll have the money wired. Will the entire team be going?"

Moretti said they would.

"I'll speak with President Liu and ask if he wants the two members of Nemesis residing in Beijing to attend," referring to General Chien An, the Chief of the General Staff of the People's Liberation Army, and Gao Hui, a member of China's Politburo Standing Committee, the decision-making body of the Chinese Communist Party.

"Their attendance may work to our advantage," Han Li said, "since no one will know they're associated with us."

"I know I'm asking the impossible, but can you both try and keep a low profile for once? There will be a multitude of media in Davos, and I don't want to answer questions on why my bean counters are sending people to the morgue."

"We'll be inconspicuous, sir," Moretti promised.

That assurance fell substantially short of what happened.

# SEVEN

Davos is a small town in the eastern Alps region of Switzerland with a population of just over eleven thousand. Getting there takes some effort. The closest airport is Altenrhein, which is forty-nine miles away. However, because of its short runway, only smaller passenger aircraft land there. Most who come to Davos land in Zurich, which is seventy-five miles from the town, and take the three-hour seventeen-minute train ride or cut that time in half by renting a car.

The Nemesis team took a United Airlines flight from Washington Dulles, landing in Zurich eight hours later at seven fifty-five in the morning—Swiss time being six hours ahead of EST. They had reservations at the Tschuggen Grand Hotel in Arosa, which was seven miles from Davos, unable to get lodging there at any price because every room was booked six months prior to the conference. Since rental vehicles were also at a premium in Zurich, and a seven-seat SUV was unavailable, the only choice they had to transport everyone together was a fifteen-seat Mercedes Benz Sprinter.

The temperature in Davos was thirty-one degrees Fahrenheit and expected to dip to fifteen at night. The team brought L.L. Bean parkas and other cold weather gear in addition to their business casual attire. The ride was uneventful with Moretti, who grew up in Anchorage, Alaska, at the wheel and maneuvering the roads in the light blowing snow like a native, pulling into the hotel's parking lot at eleven.

"This is a universe above the NCO barracks at Site R," McGough said as they entered the posh lobby.

"Don't get used to it," Moretti responded. "My experience is the pendulum swings both ways. We could be sleeping on a dirt bed in the mountains in a few weeks."

"Been there, done that. I'll take it as it comes," he responded with a smile.

Each team member presented their passport at the check-in counter and signed the registration form, after which they were handed a key. Moretti used his government credit card to pay for their rooms, which were spread throughout the hotel. As he was doing this, Han Li was on her phone.

"Gao Hui and Chien An have already checked in, and I have their room numbers," she said, joining the team near the two hotel elevators.

"Let's get cleaned up and meet in our room in thirty," Moretti replied, giving the number of the room that he and Han Li were staying in and pressing the elevator button.

Everyone nodded in agreement as an elevator door opened, and they entered.

As the team stood in front of the elevators, a man wearing a brown Gorsuch cashmere ski jacket looked at them over the top of his *Financial Times* paper. He was five feet, five inches tall, bald, of Asian descent, and carried an extra twenty pounds around his stomach. His thick, black-framed glasses had progressive lenses, allowing him to transition between distance and close vision smoothly. When the team entered the elevator, he removed the cellphone from his jacket pocket and placed a call.

Having received the information from Pruitt on the White House Statistical Analysis Division's flight and hotel arrangements, the thin man had expected the call from Davos confirming their arrival and answered on the first ring.

"Did they drive or arrive by public transport?"

The Asian said he saw them get out of a black Mercedes Benz Sprinter.

"I don't want them to know they're being watched. Text me when they leave the hotel but don't follow them." The call ended.

The Asian leaned back on the couch, ordered a double espresso, and looked toward the elevators.

The thin man was a familiar face in Davos. In the last decade and a half, he'd given enough money to politicians, law enforcement officers, and local officials—and had a relationship with several crime syndicates so that he could get or arrange for anything. One syndicate was the Albanian mafia, whose primary business in Switzerland was selling heroin and laundering that money through the restaurants, bars, real estate, and other local enterprises it owned through proxies. One of those enterprises was a snow removal company, with Canton records showing it was a subsidiary of a Zurich entity engaged in the same trade. It was purchased by the Swiss arm of the Albanian Mafia years ago. However, the person listed in government records as the sole shareholder was a Mafia proxy who took orders from the mob's leadership. That person was sitting across from the thin man, having been summoned from Zurich.

"These men work for the president of the United States," the Mafia chieftain said after hearing the thin man's request to kill Moretti and Han Li. "There will be repercussions—the type that brings immense scrutiny. The risk is too high for me to accept this contract. The Swiss government can put me out of business tomorrow if they believe I or someone working for me was involved."

"The risk is minimal if you make it appear their deaths were accidental."

"I know from experience that the appearance of an accidental death is an imperfect science. There's no such thing as the perfect murder if one looks close enough—and I expect the president will have his team do that."

"I'll double your fee," the thin man said, knowing greed was the Albanian's kryptonite.

"When does this need to happen?"

"Tonight."

"Impossible."

The thin man had negotiated with this chieftain in the past, understanding that he enjoyed haggling and tried to extract as much money as possible before agreeing. He was prepared to triple the regular contract fee but had to wait to get to that number until the chieftain tried once again to ratchet the deal higher. He found this dance tiring, but the process was culturally engrained into the person he was negotiating with. He offered triple.

"The money is not enough for the risk I'm taking."

It was time to cut to the chase. "You've left me no choice but to ask the Romas," he said, using the non-derogatory word for Gypsies.

"You can't trust a Roma. They're thieves."

"So are you."

"But in a good way," the chieftain replied with a smile, extending his hand and signaling their negotiation was over.

Each member of Nemesis had a room at the Tschuggen Grand Hotel—not because the members were opposed to sharing one, but because the rooms were small. Each was two hundred five square feet except for the South Facing Suite, which was seven hundred square feet. Moretti and Han Li took that, and the team met there to avoid gathering in a corner of the hotel lounge or restaurant and attracting attention.

The suite had two rooms—a bedroom and living room, the latter having two sofas at right angles, two club chairs, and a desk with what looked to be an uncomfortable wooden chair in front of it. Each member, including Chien An and Gao Hui, picked their spot. Han Li was the first to speak.

"You should have received a list of those who attended the forum for the past ten years," she said, referring to an email she forwarded from Alexson, which gave a detailed summary of what the techies could find on each.

Everyone acknowledged receiving it and that they could access the information from their phone.

"According to the techs," she continued, "of the approximately three thousand who attend the forum, slightly more than seven percent have returned for the past decade. This narrows our list to two hundred thirteen names. Twenty-three of those are from the United States and represent industry leaders and government functions such as the CIA, DIA, FBI, State Department, and so forth. Great Britain and China each have eighteen attendees, Russia and Germany have seventeen, France has twelve, and it goes down from there."

"I can see the State Department, but what are the FBI, DIA, and CIA doing here?" McGough asked.

"The most influential people in the world attend the World Economic Forum," Chien An replied. "Hear what they say, and you'll know that nation's political, economic, military, and other leanings. This is valuable intel when assembling a strategic model for negotiating trade and conducting other business between nations. The Politburo Standing Committee sent four representatives for those reasons. Out of the country and in these types of settings, away from public relations firms and speech writers, you'll hear what government officials, heads of corporations, and other influencers really think."

"According to his emails, Cray believes many members of the Cabal have been coming here annually since at least 2007," Moretti said. "Assuming they're here to exchange ideas, set their yearly agenda, discuss significant upcoming events, and possibly go over their finances, we need to listen to those conversations."

"There's seven of us to cull two hundred thirteen names," Bonaquist said. "This forum lasts four days. There's not enough time to verify the Cabal members. Even if we did, eavesdropping on them would be difficult because we don't know where they meet. I would also venture that their discussions are in a private location and only between members."

"Those are valid points, Jack, and problems we need to overcome," Moretti conceded. "Before we left DC, I gave the president a list of equipment we needed. Since it would raise a red flag if customs found these in our bags, I asked him to put them in diplomatic pouches to the US embassy in Bern. Thirty minutes ago, an embassy official delivered what I ordered."

"What about weapons?" Jian Shen asked.

"None. Suppose we're discovered with a weapon or are in a position where we have to fight our way out of a situation. In that case, the president will face international scrutiny as to why his analysts were armed or involved in a gunfight."

Although the team felt naked without weapons, they understood their need to be unarmed.

Moretti moved on. "We have three functions in the field. The first is to communicate effectively with one another. The second is to identify Cabal members. The third is to eavesdrop on them without being discovered. For the first function, we'll use the Molar Mic."

The Molar Mic was a tiny communications package that clipped onto the last upper molar on one side of a person's mouth. In addition, the user wore two small devices under their clothing to facilitate transmission, reception, and encryption of conversations. The system eliminated the need for headsets, earbuds, head-mounted microphones, and the wires that linked them. More importantly, they could pass through metal detectors. The built-in microphone picked up the user's voice as low as a whisper. Transmissions from others were heard by converting what they said to vibrations on one's teeth, reverberating into the middle ear. The team was familiar with it, having been briefed on its operation and given a demonstration by the manufacturer's rep, although she didn't know anything about her audience.

"That was good planning," Chien An said as Moretti brought a large box out of the bedroom and handed out the devices.

"That satisfies our first function, now for the second—identifying members of the Cabal," Moretti continued, removing boxes of smart contact lenses and handing them out. This received an enthusiastic response.

Smart contact lenses could best be compared to the lenses worn by Jeremy Renner in the movie *Mission: Impossible—Ghost Protocol*. The lightweight micro-battery-powered contacts transmitted whatever the wearer saw, continuously streaming several hours of video to the user's cellphone, which was linked to Site R. The recording started when the wearer voluntarily blinked and stopped when they did it again. A natural blink lasts 0.2 to 0.4 seconds, with a voluntary blink lasting 0.5 seconds or longer—the embedded technology distinguishing between the two. Once Alexson and Connelly received and processed the data, they'd run it through multi-national facial recognition programs and learn the identities of everyone photographed. At least, that's the way it was designed to work.

"We can now discretely speak to one another and photograph and identify those we're seeing. That gets us to the third function, eavesdropping," Moretti said. "To hear what everyone is saying, we'll use these." He removed the last items from the box and handed out what appeared to be Mont Blanc pens.

"Laser mics," Gao Hui said.

"You're all familiar with this device, but I'll review its operation again to ensure we haven't forgotten anything. If you point the tip of the pen at an object near someone who's talking and press the clip, it detects what they're saying by picking up and converting the sound vibrations from that object. The laser beam can also be directed at an object on the other side of a window. The reflected beam hits this transceiver," he said, holding up a plastic box the size of a card deck, "which converts the vibrations to an audio signal. Just as with the smart contact lenses, the data will go to your cellphone, which will be linked to Site R. It doesn't matter if they're speaking another language; the audio will be washed through a series of translation programs, depending on how many languages the computer detects."

"With everything dependent on a good cell signal, what happens if there isn't one?" Jian Shen asked.

"That's the chink in the armor. Find a location that gives you the most bars on your phone. If you don't have a good signal, move on to another person on your list. As Jack pointed out, there's no shortage of names."

"Where do we start?" McGough asked.

"Because we work for the White House, we've received invitations to several side conferences, cocktail parties, and a host of after-hours social events. Although the forum starts tomorrow, the social gatherings begin tonight. Not all are in Davos. Some are in adjoining towns. I believe Jack is right in believing the Cabal members meet privately. If we discover that location, we can at least get photos of their members and possibly figure out how to monitor their conversations. There's also the possibility they attend outside functions. When we're there, we may pick up chatter about their meetings or the suspicious activities of some of the attendees. We need to take an aggressive posture if we're going to make something happen in four days. Therefore, we're going to attend as many events as possible."

Moretti turned to Chien An and Guo Hui. "Since no one knows your association with us, we'll keep it that way. You'll attend two functions this evening away from where the rest of us will be," he said, telling them the events they were attending and handing them a slip of paper with their locations. After he directed where the others would go, everyone left the room. They assumed what they were about to do would be significantly less risky than hunting terrorists and those who wanted to make a statement by destroying something they shouldn't or killing innocents. They were also prepared for the mind-numbing tedium of electronic stakeouts. None anticipated what would happen, nor that the next time the team assembled, not everyone would be present.

# EIGHT

The Asian man was sitting at a table with a cold cup of espresso in front of him, watching the front door for Moretti, Han Li, and those who entered the hotel with them. Their photos were on his cell phone, and he periodically looked at them to keep their faces fresh in his mind. At first, he paid no attention to Chien An and Gao Hui, but that changed when Moretti went to the front desk to get a detailed map of Davos and Gao Hui spotted him. He came over and hugged the ex-Ranger—whispering in his ear that he and Chien An were wearing their smart contact lenses, although the Asian had no idea what was said. However, it cemented the notion they knew one another and were associated with the group accompanying Moretti and Han Li.

Lifting his cellphone off the table, he took photos of Chien An and Gao Hui and sent them to the thin man. Seconds later, he received a text telling him to include them in the group he was watching. What the Asian didn't know was that he wasn't the only person the thin man had at the hotel. Outside in the parking lot, he had operatives whose assignments were to follow Moretti, Han Li, and those who arrived with them. He added Chien An and Gao Hui to that list.

Gao Hui, Chien An, and the other Chinese attendees at the forum were invited to virtually every social gathering because of

71

their status within the Chinese government. The end game for those inviting them was to gain entry or expand their presence into a market with a billion and a half potential customers whose annual income continued to rise, get China to finance one or more of their homeland projects, or get them to buy their country's exports. They had numerous attractive hostesses and briefcases of cash to help them attain one or more of these goals.

Since the conference rooms and venues in Davos were consistently booked during the week of the World Economic Forum, nearby towns cashed in on this windfall by satisfying the considerable demand for meeting space. As a result, the social gathering that Gao Hui and Chien An were attending was in Igis, a small town twenty-seven miles from Davos. The second event they would go to that evening was in Chur, seven miles from Igis.

Their first function was hosted by an African country that wanted foreign investment so it could increase its natural resource production and exports. Even though the invites didn't disclose this was the purpose of the gathering, everyone with knowledge of the country knew that was their intent. Since China was aggressively pushing its agenda in Africa, and domestic natural resources were in short supply, Gao Hui and Chien An knew that every Chinese attendee would be there to expand their government interests, gain valuable intelligence data, and close a deal. The country sponsoring the event in Chur had a different reason for inviting the Chinese. They were transitioning from petroleum to solar and wind energy. Because China manufactured solar panels and wind turbines, they wanted to negotiate a deal that came with financing.

The road to Igis had two inches of snow on it, and because some melted earlier from the sunshine and traffic and refroze from the cold wind, the road was icy and going slow. Chien An was driving and, having spent a fair amount of time in the northern border area of China, was a pro in this type of weather. Behind their vehicle was the Volvo S90 sedan, which had been tailing them since leaving the hotel. He didn't know whether they were also going to Igis, but the fact that the Volvo maintained its distance, despite changing his speed by as much as twenty mph, made him lean in the direction of a tail. He decided to call Moretti and tell him that according to their GPS, they were within five minutes of their destination. He unbuckled the seatbelt to get at the phone in his pocket.

Unfastening one's seatbelt in a moving car is never a good idea. Statistically, one is twenty-five times more likely to die when ejected from a vehicle than staying inside. However, in this situation, being thrown through the front window and out of their VW Tiguan saved his life when a snowplow/sander truck, which was a dump truck with a snowplow in front and a sand spreader in the rear, came out of nowhere and slammed into the right-rear of the vehicle. The mismatch resulted in the VW doing a ninety-degree turn to the left and going over the embankment. Chien An flew through the front window, narrowly avoiding striking one of the numerous trees nearby or being crushed by the tumbling Tiguan. Gao Hui, strapped within the vehicle, survived the crash thanks to the three airbags deploying around him.

The Tiguan came to rest upright fifty yards below the embankment, ricocheting off several trees as it rolled. Although the vehicle's roof and sides were crushed, the VW engineers did a great job protecting those within. However, their algorithms probably didn't consider a fifty-eight thousand seven hundred forty pound truck slamming into the three thousand eight hundred fifty-six pound vehicle.

Once the Tiguan flew over the embankment, the snowplow and the Volvo stopped at the edge of the road, their drivers getting out of the vehicles and looking over the side. Because it was nighttime, neither could see the Tiguan. Since their orders were to kill both persons in the vehicle, the snowplow driver took two flashlights from his truck and handed one to the driver of the Volvo as they wordlessly started down the hill.

They immediately sank to their knees in the snow; in some areas, it was so deep it came to their thighs. Neither saw Chien An, stepping past the unconscious general who was two-thirds of the way to the Tiguan and covered in snow.

When the drivers reached the vehicle, they shined their lights inside and saw that Gao Hui was still alive and not seriously injured. However, the crushed car wedged him tightly inside so he couldn't get out.

"Where's the other person?" the Volvo driver asked as he shone his light around the vehicle.

"He was thrown from the car. He's dead. No one survives going through a windshield."

"The thin man told us to make this look like an accident. We can't put a bullet in him or slit his throat."

"I have an idea," the snowplow driver replied. Removing the gas cap from the mangled vehicle, he rolled his handkerchief into a tight rope, inserted one end into the gas tank, and lit the end. He didn't have to tell the other driver to run because he was already a dozen steps away.

The explosion was massive, sending pieces of the vehicle in every direction.

"Let's search for the other person to make sure he's dead," the Volvo driver said.

"There's no time. He could be anywhere. Someone will have heard the explosion or see the fire. It won't be long before this place crawls with police and rescue vehicles. We need to get out of here."

"The thin man won't like that we didn't confirm the other person's death."

"If someone sees us, we won't have to worry about what he likes or dislikes; we'll be the next casualties."

They returned to their vehicles and left.

Chien An had regained consciousness and saw what had happened. He watched Gao Hui's killers walk within a foot of him and, without a weapon, kept silent as they passed and trudged up the hill. When they were out of sight, he ran to the Tiguan.

A passing motorist saw the flames not long after the killers left and notified authorities. Ten minutes later, the police and an ambulance arrived within seconds of each other. When they arrived, the paramedics found Chien An shivering from the cold as he stood staring at the charred remains of his friend. They couldn't believe he only had facial cuts and bruises when he told them the crash sent him through the vehicle's front window.

He told police that a snowplow blindsided their vehicle and, because at that moment he unfastened his seatbelt to get his cellphone, the impact threw him from the car. His story was confirmed when the police saw heavy truck tracks leading to the embankment and took plaster casts of them.

The police drove Chien An back to the hotel, the officers trying to make him feel better by saying they'd find whoever was responsible and put them behind bars. As far as the general was concerned, that wasn't going to happen because he had no intention of returning to China without finding and killing those responsible.

Not long after Chien An and Gao Hui left the hotel for Igis, the rest of the Nemesis team walked through the lobby and went outside. As they did, the Asian texted the thin man and notified him of their departure, receiving a thumbs-up emoji in return.

The team walked to the Mercedes Benz Sprinter, which was in the far corner of the parking lot in one of several spaces reserved for vehicles that size. As they did, two of the thin man's operatives watched from a black Mercedes C 300. When the Sprinter left the lot, they followed.

Because it was night, and no one checked beneath the vehicle, the small amount of brake fluid on the snow went unnoticed. The person who loosened the nut on the brake fluid line was an expert at adjusting the precise amount of leakage needed so that the brakes would fail in a specific area. In this situation, he loosened the line so that its brakes would fail as it was on the winding mountainous descent to the main highway, which was several miles from the hotel.

Moretti saw the brake warning light flash red on his instrument panel shortly after the road peaked at the top of the mountain and began its winding descent to the highway. Believing he was low on brake fluid, he confirmed this by taping the brakes lightly and noticing the pedal was slightly closer to the floorboard. He immediately downshifted to low gear, causing everyone's restraint straps to tighten as their bodies were thrown forward.

"We're losing our brakes," Moretti yelled so those in the back could hear. "Tighten your belts because this will be a wild ride to the highway."

Han Li, seated in the passenger seat beside him, asked how she could help.

"Hold on tight because I just lost the last of my brakes," Moretti said as he continued to pump the pedal without getting a response.

The Sprinter began to accelerate, with Moretti barely able to hold it on the twisting unlit road that abruptly descended downward. Seconds later, the right tires came off the pavement. Bonaquist and McGough felt what was happening and, instinctively knowing what needed to be done, unbuckled their seat belts and went to the opposite side of the vehicle. Their combined weight of nearly five hundred fifty pounds brought the right tires back onto the pavement.

"How far to the highway?" McGough asked.

"Too far."

"That's what I thought," the Force Recon Marine said as he returned to his seat and tightened the straps until they hurt.

The Sprinter was on a barrierless unlit mountain road with a steep five thousand feet deep valley to the left and the side of a mountain to the right. There was no traffic —at least none that Moretti could see because the road twisted so extensively that the headlights only showed the area between the vehicle and the next twist. His only option was to brush the side of the mountain, hoping the friction would slow the Sprinter down until it eventually stopped. However, the problem was the large outcroppings sporadically jutting from the mountain. Hitting one of these would careen and redirect the vehicle sharply to the left, catapulting it off the highway and into the steep valley. But if he didn't brush the mountain, he'd lose control of the vehicle because of his excessive speed, or the inevitable destruction of the gearbox made control of the Sprinter impossible. Either would send him off the highway. It wasn't much of a choice.

As Moretti told everyone to brace themselves because he would be scraping the side of the mountain, there was a catastrophic mechanical failure as the gearbox threw in the towel. The vehicle's values contacted the pistons due to valve float, the clutches exploded due to G-forces, the internal engine parts ejected through the block, and valve and clutch parts burst through the hood. As this happened, Moretti pulled the wheel to the right and into the mountain. However, scraping the side of the mountain didn't slow the vehicle. Instead, the contact resulted in it veering uncontrollably to the left and flipping the three-ton Sprinter on its side, followed by eight somersaults before it came to rest two feet from the edge of the valley-side of the road.

The Mercedes C 300, which kept well behind the Sprinter so as not to get too close as it went into its death throes, saw the battered vehicle on its side at the edge of the road. The question they had was: how many survived? Because this was supposed to look like an accident, they couldn't take the automatic rifles from their trunk and spray the inside of the vehicle with bullets to ensure there were no survivors. Instead, all they could do was check it and report back. Twenty seconds later, they had company when a taxi returning a guest to the hotel stopped behind the wreck, which blocked its side of the road. The driver and passenger raced from the car, the four arriving at the demolished Sprinter simultaneously.

The taxi driver summoned emergency vehicles, which arrived within twelve minutes, and the Nemesis team was taken to Spitex, the Davos hospital providing twenty-four-hour emergency care. Because the Mercedes was a heavy vehicle that took the pounding well, and they were wearing seat belts with shoulder harnesses, everyone survived. Moretti and Han Li suffered multiple bruises, their faces struck by deploying airbags. Bonaquist sustained a cut over his right eye, which required four stitches after a jagged piece of metal hit him. Jian Shen was gashed when the left side of his seat tore loose and sliced into his thigh—requiring fifteen stitches. Remarkably, those were the only injuries. The other members of the team, who didn't have the benefit of an airbag, were shielded by the heavy exterior of the vehicle and had only bruises and cuts from the somersaulting vehicle's eight impacts with the ground and flying glass.

Released from the hospital, they took taxis back to the hotel and entered the lobby, finding Chien An sitting at a table in the lounge with a tall drink in front of him. Cuts and bruises on his face, and the absence of Gao Hui, told them the unthinkable had happened.

McGough pulled an adjoining table next to the one where Chien An was sitting, and the rest of the team brought over the chairs. Everyone took a seat.

"Where is Gao Hui?" Moretti asked.

In response to the question, Chien An meticulously recounted what happened from when they left the hotel until his return. "I called President Liu, who said he'd tell President Ballinger. The Chinese embassy in Bern is arranging for his transport to Beijing."

"I think we can rule out the brake failure as accidental," Moretti said. "The Cabal is not just going after Cray; they're also going after us."

"How could anyone know you both were associated with us? The only place the team met was in our room," Han Li asked.

"That's not true," Moretti answered. "I spoke to Chien An in the lobby prior to them leaving for Igis. Someone must have seen us."

"Which means they have a spy in the hotel," McGough said, looking around. As he did, everyone followed his gaze, which settled on an Asian man sipping coffee at a nearby table.

"I noticed him there when we checked in and left," Han Li said.

"I wonder if he's a guest?" Bonaquist asked.

"Let me find out," Moretti said. He returned five minutes later. "The twenty euro answer from the waiter is that, when he asked for the man's room number, he said he wasn't staying at the hotel and paid cash. Maybe Alexson and Connely can tell us about him," he said, looking in his direction and blinking—taking a photo of the Asian with his smart contact lens.

When Alexson and Connelly received the image from Moretti, they began by running it through the US government's facial recognition databases and, when it went unrecognized, put it through those of its allies, also not getting a hit. They then hacked into the facial recognition databases of other nations, something they'd done in the past using the sophisticated software tools of their former employer, the NSA. Ultimately, they verified the identity of the Asian as Kadeem Malik, born in Lahore, Pakistan, and living in Zurich, which had a large Pakistani community. Once they had his name, they looked at the guests staying at the various hotels in the Davos area, finding he was at the AlpenGold Hotel in Davos, although sipping coffee at the Tschuggen Hotel in Arosa. They then checked his name against those attending the World Economic Forum, discovering he wasn't one of the attendees. Because the hotel he was staying in wasn't cheap, especially during the forum, the techs wondered what he was doing in Davos this time of year and how he earned his living. They found the answer on his tax return, which listed his occupation as a security consultant. That meant he was an independent contractor since Swiss employees are taxed on a pay-as-you-earn system arranged by their employers, while self-employed workers submit a tax return annually.

"There's one more thing you should know," Moretti said after the techs informed him of what they found, telling them what happened to the team and Gao Hui's death.

The news of Gao's death hit techs hard. Although they'd only met him twice, they spoke with the affable member of Nemesis two to three times a week, receiving data on persons of interest that only existed in China's databases.

"The team will make this right," Alexson said to Connelly once the call ended, both agreeing that whoever killed Gao Hui better do some quick estate planning, knowing what Chien An did to the person who killed Yan He, the last Nemesis member to be killed in the field.

"We need to look at the images Gao sent us from his smart contact lens," Connelly said, the techs waiting to process the data until they spoke with him to see if these were operational images or a quick test of the system, which was possible since it was the first time he'd used smart contact lens in the field.

Following the same procedures they'd used with Moretti's image, they brought up the images Gao Hui sent, knowing that the two persons they were looking at were his executioners. Skipping the US facial recognition databases, they went straight to the Swiss system and identified Kushrim Fega and Bastien Wyss. The Swiss database showed Fega was a snow removal and road maintenance supervisor for the Canton of Graubünden, which included Davos. According to his tax return, Wyss was an independent driver working for a transportation company in Zurich. They next looked at where they lived or were staying.

Alexson called Moretti and sent him the photos and data on the two individuals, including that Wyss was staying at the AlpenGold Hotel in Davos, the same as Malik, and the address of Fega's residence.

While Alexson and Connelly were processing Gao Hui's data, the team cleaned up and put on fresh clothes in their rooms. One by one, they trickled downstairs and returned to the same table where they'd sat with Chien An. When the last person arrived, Moretti put his cellphone in the center of the table so everyone could see Gao Hui's photos of the two who'd killed him. He then went over the data that Alexson and Connelly sent, with the looks on everyone's faces being revenge-driven determination to find his killers.

"We're going to have a very unpleasant conversation with Malik, Fega, and Wyss to find out he hired them and what they know," Moretti said, displaying his anger. "We know that Malik and Wyss are staying at the AlpenGold Hotel in Davos and that Fega has a house not far from Chur."

Looking at Google Earth, they saw Fega lived in a small house in a wooded area where the nearest neighbor was several hundred yards away.

"We can interrogate Fega at his house this evening and bring Malik and Wyss there and see what they know," Han Li said.

"That's a good idea," Bonaquist conceded, "but we'll need a vehicle, and we don't have any weapons. We could have a serious problem if even one of these three do."

"Maybe someone can loan us a couple of vehicles," Moretti said.

"Who would be that crazy?"

"The US government."

"What about the weapons? We don't have them because we didn't want to invite questions about why the president's analysts were armed," Bonaquist continued.

"The rules have changed, and if we don't want to join Gao Hui, the gloves need to come off. Our primary mission is to uncover the Cabal's members, learn what they're planning, and discover why they targeted Cray. I'm not averse to planting a few of their members in the ground to find that out."

"We're getting weapons?" Chien An asked.

"Lots of them."

# NINE

The three employees from the US consulate in Zurich weren't happy when told they were driving to Arosa, leaving two Ford Excursions at the Tschuggen Hotel, and returning in the third. The reason for this state of mind was that it meant they couldn't attend a late-evening party at the French consulate, which was renowned for fantastic food, expensive beverages, and Cuban cigars. In the backs of the Ford Excursions were massive amounts of weaponry and supplies that had been helicoptered one hundred sixty-five miles from the US Army base in Baumholder, Germany, to Zurich.

The drive took slightly under two hours. The seven thousand six hundred pound vehicles, each carrying weapons that added substantially to their weight, gripped the snowy road as surely as if they were on summertime asphalt. The three consulate employees arrived at the hotel at one in the morning. As they approached the registration desk, they saw a large burly man leave a group seated at a long table to the side of the lobby. By this time the Asian man, who believed it would be conspicuous if he stayed too late, had departed.

Introductions were made. "We'll accompany you to the vehicles so you can inspect what we brought," one driver said. "But before then, restrooms?"

He pointed, and the three made a beeline. After they returned and made to-go cups of coffee from the urn in the lobby, Moretti followed them to the Excursions, which had diplomatic license plates, and looked at the arms in the cargo area. He liked having the plates, which gave the team significant latitude because law enforcement couldn't stop them for traffic violations or search the cars.

After signing for the vehicles and weapons, he returned to the hotel lobby and rejoined the team.

"Is everything there?" Han Li asked.

"God loves the Army. They must have thought we were going to Afghanistan and gave us a few weapons that weren't on our list," Moretti said, handing her a copy of the receipt he'd signed. After looking at it, she passed it to Bonaquist, and it made its way to the other team members.

"Now we're talking," Shen said. "We're not coming out number two with this firepower."

"That's a double-edged sword," Moretti cautioned. "If we get into a public shooting match, our time in Switzerland is over, and our mission will have failed. We'll only use these weapons outside of public view."

Everyone acknowledged the rules of engagement.

"Where do we start?" Bonaquist asked.

"With Mr. Fega," Moretti said. "He has some explaining to do."

With that remark, the team got up from the table, put on their parkas, and went to the vehicles.

The team went to the Excursions, and each grabbed a Glock 20, which was in a shoulder holster, a silencer, a flashlight, several spare fifteen-round capacity magazines, and night vision goggles. After putting the address of Fega's residence into the GPS of one of the vehicles, they left the hotel and retraced their route to the highway over the same mountain road they'd driven earlier, the Excursion sticking to it like glue, even though it'd become icy.

At two a.m., the vehicle pulled into an unlit area thirty yards off the road and two hundred yards from Fega's house. With the neighborhood devoid of streetlights, the team wore their night vision goggles as they trekked through ankle-deep snow to the rear of the residence. Although nearby houses had porch lamps, none of that light found Fega's home, which was pitch black because the cloud cover also extinguished the glow from the quarter moon.

The house was nothing to brag about. Whatever money Fega made in the Albanian Mafia and plowing roads wasn't going into his one thousand square feet, one-bedroom home two miles from Chur. The aging structure was forty years old. During that time, judging from the warped decking, faded paint, and patched roof with three shades of shingles, it had undergone minimalistic repairs to keep it functionally dilapidated. If the team had questioned his neighbors, they would have learned that they reviled the Albanian because of the condition of his home and his ambivalence to maintaining it. Even though his neighbors' houses were pristine, the eyesore impacted their value and made them nearly impossible to sell. Although it wasn't all that close to Fega's home, the residence next door had been on the market for a year before the owner threw up his hands, pulled the sign, and called it a day.

The plan was for Moretti, Han Li, and Chien An to enter through the front door while Bonaquist, Jian Shen, and McGough went through the rear. In preparation, each person screwed their silencer onto their weapon. Communicating through his molar mics, Han Li picked the lock on the front door while McGough did the same in the back. Because the locks were cheap and had deteriorated over the years, they were inside within seconds. Converging to the bedroom, they found Fega asleep and snoring soundly, an empty bottle of schnapps and two porn magazines on the floor beside the bed. Moretti clamped his large hand over the scumbag's mouth and simultaneously put his gun to his forehead—waking the killer with a start.

"Make a sound, and I'll put a very large hole in your head," Moretti said in a threatening voice, believing the scumbag, feeling a gun barrel pressed hard against his forehead, would understand his intent whether or not he spoke English.

"Goggles up, and someone turn on the bedroom light," Moretti ordered.

Bonaquist found the switch and turned on the ceiling light. The room, which had dirty clothes littering the floor from one end to the other, along with a couple of empty pizza boxes and Chinese food containers, had an odor the team would later say reminded them of a restaurant dumpster.

"What do you want?" Fega asked, betraying that he spoke English.

Moretti didn't answer. Instead, he dragged the gangster to a chair, secured him to it with his dirty clothes, and gagged him with a t-shirt that had once been white but was now light charcoal. "I'm going to ask you a few questions," he said, "after which I'll remove your gag and listen to your answer. If I believe it, we'll go on to the next question. If I suspect you're lying, you won't like my response. Let's give it a shot. "First question. Who hired you?"

Moretti removed the gag, immediately after which Fega looked at him defiantly and spat in his direction. However, since his mouth was dry, the spit landed on his knee.

"You need an attitude adjustment," he said, replacing the gag. Then, without warning, he violently planted his boot in the gangster's groin. This elicited a scream that would have awoken the entire neighborhood had it not been for the gag. Thirty seconds later, when the muffled cries of pain subsided, he calmly removed the gag and re-asked the question, resting his boot on a strategic part of the scumbag's anatomy. No sooner had he done this than the Albanian told him that the thin man hired him.

"That's not a name; it's a description. What's his name?"

"I've never heard anyone say his name."

"Why did he want you to kill the people in that vehicle?"

"He didn't say, and I didn't ask. It was a contract."

"How do I find the thin man?"

"Look for the biggest house in Davos."

The questioning continued for another fifteen minutes. They learned he worked for the Albanian Mafia and did whatever he was told. They paired him on this hit with Bastien Wyss, who he identified as another Mafia member whose job was to follow Chien An and Gao Hui's Tiguan and continually give him their position. He also knew Kadeen Malik, who the team referred to as the Asian.

Moretti left the scumbag and went to the other members of his team at the back of the bedroom.

"We've gotten all we're going to get from him," Moretti said. "The big question is: how we get Wyss and Malik here to interrogate them?"

"I have an idea," Han Li said, taking Fega's phone off the nightstand and asking him how he contacted Wyss and Malik. Not believing Han Li was a threat, he ignored the question and gave her a defiant look. That look of defiance stayed on his face for less than a second before Han Li, faster than the blink of an eye, delivered a throat strike that hit his windpipe, impacting the carotid baroreceptor and vagus nerve, sending a paralyzing pain throughout his body that impaired his breathing. It took five minutes for Fega to speak. When he did, his second attitude adjustment resulted in Wyss and Malik's phone numbers. Han Li took his phone and texted each, telling them to come immediately to Fega's house.

Wyss and Malik drove together, contacting each other after receiving the texts from Fega. Although he didn't mention the thin man, both knew they wouldn't be summoned in the middle of the night unless Fega received instructions from him.

When they arrived at the house and knocked on the door, McGough and Jian Shen opened it and pulled them inside. Neither was carrying a weapon. Both were questioned, with Malik saying he was summoned from Zurich to monitor their movements and Wyss telling them his job was to follow whoever left the hotel.

"What if we went in separate directions?"

"There are others outside your hotel."

"No one followed us tonight."

"There's a gap when it's assumed you're asleep. They'll be there at six."

"Tell us what you know about the Cabal?"

Looking at the faces of the three in front of him, Moretti knew the answer to his question before each said they didn't know what he was talking about. He rejoined his team. "They're low-level thugs," he said.

"What do we do with them?" Bonaquist asked.

"They killed Gao Hui. We can't let that slide," Jian Shen said.

As everyone offered an opinion on what to do with the three, Chien An ended those discussions by putting a bullet in each of their heads.

"That problem seems to be solved," Moretti said, breaking the silence. "We need to get back to the hotel while it's still dark. Let's torch the place to get rid of any forensic evidence like hair fibers."

"The police won't waste too much time investigating when they learn these three were members of the Albanian Mafia. They'll think it was a dispute among rivals," Chien An said.

Everyone agreed with that assumption, setting the house on fire before they left.

It was nearly 5 a.m. when they parked the Ford Excursion and entered the hotel. They were dragging after surviving the car crash, going to the hospital, the emotional turmoil of confronting the scumbags, and a severe lack of sleep. As they headed towards the elevators, two officers from the Graubünden Canton police force, as each canton was responsible for its law enforcement, approached Moretti and Han Li with their weapons drawn. Ignoring everyone else, they told them they were under arrest and to get down on their knees and interlace their fingers on their heads.

"On what charges?" Moretti asked as one officer frisked him before moving on to Han Li, wondering how the police could have discovered what they did so quickly and why they were the only two under arrest. If there was a silver lining, it was that they left their weapons in the vehicle, and neither of them drove to the hotel and had the car keys on them.

"Unlawful flight to avoid prosecution for murder and attempted murder, in violation of Title 18, section 1073 of the US Code," the officer said, reading from one of the warrants.

"How is that a violation of Swiss law?" Moretti asked.

"Your FBI issued the warrants and requested your extradition back to the US." As he said this, his partner handcuffed and pulled them to their feet, escorting them out of the hotel and into the cold winter air.

As Moretti and Han Li were on their way to the police station, Samuel Bradford phoned Gillespie and informed him of the arrest. "Does the president know?" he asked.

"Not yet. Only the director, who informed the thin man. He'll ensure their arrests don't appear in the President's Daily Brief. But it's only a matter of time until POTUS finds out. When he does, the extradition process will already be underway, and it will be politically untenable for him to interfere."

"What's the next step?"

"The State Department's Office of International Affairs needs to draw up the extradition request and present it to the Swiss government through diplomatic channels. I'm coordinating that now."

"When will they return to the States?"

"It depends on if they challenge their extradition. If they do, it'll take months because the process necessitates a court proceeding in Switzerland, after which an executive authority will decide whether the extradition is warranted," Bradford answered.

"We don't know what they told the other analysts. We can't take a chance that they'll expose us."

"I've come to the same conclusion," Bradford said. "Very shortly, the White House Statistical Analysis Division will have five job openings."

# TEN

Moretti and Han Li were driven to Chur, the capital of the Graubünden Canton, and booked into the Cazis Tignez prison. After officials recorded their vital information, including their name, contact information, and alleged crime, they took their fingerprints and mug shots. Following a full-body search and health check, they were allowed to dress and wear their clothing, minus personal items, and taken to a cell.

Moretti was put in a two-person six-by-eight-foot cell with a metal bunk bed. His roommate, a lifer who stood three inches taller and was a hundred pounds heavier than him, occupied the bottom bunk. He had the cell to himself for five years because he'd killed his last two cellmates. Since Switzerland doesn't have a death penalty, and life in prison was as much as they could do to this whack job, prison officials separated him from the population—until the warden received the paperwork from a senior government official to put Moretti in his cell. That official was the ultimate governing authority for the Canton's prisons. However, the idea of putting him in a cell with this type of individual came from the FBI director, who said that he and Han Li should share a cell with the worst criminals in the prison, which would *soften them up* and force their cooperation. The warden didn't have a problem with the request. If the Americans wanted their prisoners battered around a bit, or worse, then so be it. As a result, he documented their pairings were randomly assigned because of prison overcrowding.

Han Li experienced the same booking procedure and was in a duplicate six-by-eight-foot cell. Her roommate, a Russian basketball player who tipped the scale at three hundred fifty pounds because she no longer had to watch her weight or exercise, was serving a twenty-year sentence for drug smuggling. She was in her cell for only five minutes when the svelte Russian said she was her bitch and tried to seal their union by throwing her on the lower bunk and laying on top. However, that plan took a detour when Han Li elbowed her in the face and, when she dropped to her knees, snap kicked her nose—breaking it and putting the Russian out for the count.

Moretti's roommate similarly went postal but waited until night to attack, pulling him from his bunk and onto the floor. As the lifer raised his foot to stomp Moretti's face, the ex-Ranger kicked his attacker in the knee and, when he doubled over and fell, pulled the sheet off the bottom bunk, wrapped it around his attacker's neck, and twisted the other end around the steel post on the upper bunk. He then pushed down on the lifer's shoulders, tightening the noose.

"Unless you want to commit suicide, you'll give me the name of the person who told you to attack me."

The lifer, realizing he was close to being strangled, frantically waved his hand to signal he wanted to talk. Moretti stopped pushing. "One of the guards," he answered in a hoarse voice.

"What did you get in return?"

"Drugs."

"What's the guard's name?"

The lifer gave it to him.

President Ballinger was a Midwesterner. He was friendly, polite, and gave people the benefit of the doubt—traits ingrained in him from growing up in the small town of Salina, Kansas.

However, those traits had practical limits. When Bonaquist called and told him what happened to Moretti and Han Li, and that the FBI issued warrants for their arrest without telling him, he lost it. It was midnight when he called the Attorney General and FBI director, saying that he wanted to see them and that the Secret Service would pick them up in ten minutes.

After receiving the call, the FBI director phoned Bradford, who was still awake and reading the stack of paperwork he'd taken home.

"What does the president want?" Bradford asked.

"He didn't say. He wants to see the Attorney General and me."

"It must be about the warrants. He can't do anything, especially after we spin the story so everyone believes they're guilty."

"He can fire me, you, and anyone else in the government."

"But he won't. It would be political suicide," Bradford answered. In the background, he heard someone from the director's security detail telling him that a Secret Service vehicle was there to take him to the White House.

"I have to go. I'll let you know how it turns out."

When the Secret Service escorted the Attorney General and FBI director into the Oval Office, Ballinger remained seated behind his desk and dispensed with the niceties of having coffee or tea waiting, which would typically accompany a visit at such an hour.

"Why wasn't I informed beforehand that warrants were going to be issued for the arrest of Moretti and Han Li since they work for me?" the president asked as his visitors sat.

In response, the Attorney General said he knew nothing about the warrants and turned to the director, putting him on the hot seat.

"The FBI has the authority to issue warrants without consulting the Attorney General or the executive branch of government. It's called separation of powers." In other words, the president could stuff it.

"The separation is between the executive, judicial, and legislative branches," the president corrected. "In case you've forgotten, everyone in the executive branch, directly or indirectly, works for me."

The Attorney General, whose mouth gaped slightly upon hearing the director's remarks, rebounded and said he was mad that he wasn't told. "I'll add, in case you've forgotten, that the FBI is an agency of the Department of Justice, and you report to me."

"Protocols were followed," the FBI director said in response, not the least bit apologetic and implying to the Attorney General could also stuff it.

"Those protocols are from this moment changed. I now require the FBI to notify the Attorney General of all warrants and have the Department of Justice concur before going to a judge for signature."

"That's too time-consuming and burdensome."

"It's my call, not yours. Let's go over the circumstances where you felt warrants were necessary for the arrests of Moretti and Han Li," the Attorney General said, giving the FBI director a look that a principal might give an errant student. "Briefly pulling them from my system after the president phoned me, I see they were charged with unlawful flight to avoid prosecution."

"That's correct. They lured the killer they hired to murder Lieutenant Colonel Cray at the airport to his hospital room, killed him to keep their secret, and concocted a story that he was there to make a second attempt on Cray's life," the director responded.

"That's a lot of assumptions. What's your proof?"

"They killed the person in Cray's room."

"Did they? The autopsy report shows he died of renal failure. He had bad kidneys. There's no evidence of foul play. There's also no evidence he was the shooter who attempted to kill Lieutenant Colonel Cray."

"That's because Moretti took the gun case with the weapon from his vehicle. A hospital surveillance camera in the parking garage shows this."

"I saw the video, and it doesn't show what was inside the case he removed from the vehicle," the president said.

"It looks like a briefcase to me. Yet, you're assuming there was a rifle inside," the Attorney General stated.

The director remained silent.

"Explain how you can issue warrants for unlawful flight to avoid prosecution when the state of Virginia hasn't charged them with the death of the person in Cray's hospital room. The autopsy has conclusively found that he died of natural causes. Also, how do you know someone wasn't trying to kill Moretti and Han Li and not Cray at the airport?"

The director had an insolent look on his face. "Cray is a federal employee. The FBI has charged them; the state of Virginia isn't involved."

"Charged them with questionable circumstantial evidence that a first-year law student could get dismissed. An autopsy showed the man died of natural causes and, for all you know, there could have been a bag of popcorn in his briefcase."

"A judge signed the warrants."

"When's the last time you couldn't get a warrant signed by a judge? Let me answer that: never. If one judge doesn't sign it, you go to the next, and so on. There's always going to be a judge who will sign a warrant."

"I'll tighten our internal procedures for obtaining a warrant if that makes you happy," the director said arrogantly, devoid of contriteness.

"No, you won't," the Attorney General said, becoming uncharacteristically angry. "You serve at my pleasure and that of the president." Looking in his direction, he received a nod. "We have no confidence in your ability to manage the Bureau. Don't return to your office; we'll send your items to your home. You're fired."

The paperwork rescinding the warrants arrived at the Canton's police headquarters an hour and fifteen minutes after the Attorney General informed the Deputy Director that he was the acting director of the FBI until the Senate could approve a replacement. Moretti and Han Li were taken from their cells and brought to the discharge station, where the items previously taken from them were returned. They were then escorted to the front of the building and into a police vehicle, which would return them to their hotel.

"Any excitement in your cell?" Moretti asked as they sat in the back of the vehicle.

"Other than someone trying to kill me, which is normal on our deployments, no. You?"

"The same. But he gave me the name of the guard who ordered him to kill me."

"Who told the guard?"

"That question is on my checklist." As he said this, Moretti received a call from President Ballinger informing him that he and Han Li were no longer fugitives and that the Attorney General had fired the FBI director.

Their conversation continued until they reached the hotel, after which they got cleaned up and called the other team members, asking them to come to their room. Once everyone was present, they described their prison ordeal and the call with the president.

"Are we back to surveilling the conference gatherings?" Chien An asked.

"Fega may have given us a shortcut by telling us about the thin man. Although we don't know his name, he owns the largest house in Davos," Moretti said.

"How do we find it?" Jian Shen asked.

"Ask a local."

They did.

The thin man was unaccustomed to failure. Cray and the rest of the White House team were supposed to be dead. Instead, the only casualties were his contract killer, two Albanian thugs, and one of his security staff from Zurich. Rubbing salt in this wound, they escaped being killed in prison, which should have been a layup. Because the Bureau was an essential component of his new world order, his day worsened when told that the FBI director was fired. Although Bradford was still at the Bureau, he wouldn't be as effective without the director providing him with cover.

Sitting behind his desk in his underground office, he wondered how two people could be so lucky. That's when it struck him. Luck had nothing to do with it. Instead, it was their skills. How else would one explain their survival? Once he made this assumption, he made another—that they were covert operatives. This was the only reasonable explanation for how they killed Richardson, Fega, and the others. The only pieces of the puzzle that didn't fit were the two senior Chinese officials, who were too old to be operatives. Although one was dead, he needed to figure out their roles.

Everyone in Davos knew the thin man's house, and the first person asked gave directions for getting there. Taking both Excursions, they parked on the side of a mountain road and trekked through the snow until they reached an unobstructed view of the impressive residence. The gated enclave was on a large plot of land with a single access road leading from the gate to the mansion. The mountain behind it functionally protected the rear of the house because anyone attempting to sneak onto the property from that direction needed to cross an area devoid of trees or other cover, making it difficult to go unnoticed in the untracked snow. If they made it to the ten feet high stone wall surrounding the enclave, they'd encounter video surveillance and a sophisticated perimeter alarm. Coming from the other three sides was no picnic either because, after going over the wall, they'd trigger the same perimeter alarm system and be in the open until reaching the residence, the thirty feet tall windows allowing anyone inside to see them easily.

Moretti planned to get as close as possible to the mansion, using the trees as cover. The team would then peer through the floor-to-ceiling glass windows, using their high magnification scopes, to see who was inside. To get a photo or video, each would press their cellphone camera to the front of their scope and begin filming. The images wouldn't be perfect because the scope's view was circular, and the camera had a rectangular field of vision. Also, since the scope had etched reticles, those crosshairs would be in every image. However, each team member had done this before and found this technique worked well when they didn't have a camera with a telephoto lens. This time was no exception.

"I don't think there are any carbs in his diet," Moretti said as he snapped his photo. His attention then diverted to the front gate, which opened for an approaching Mercedes S580. The team didn't know the identities of the two men who exited the vehicle but were able to get clear shots of their faces. Moretti sent them, and the photo of the thin man, to Alexson to run through the government's facial recognition databases. Five minutes later, he received Eugene Gillespie and Adam Tanner's names and summary information. The thin man took ten minutes longer to identify, the techs finding that he had a British passport with the name Tenant Masterson.

"What is the Deputy Director of the National Clandestine Service arm of the CIA and the Director of the military intelligence staff for the Defense Intelligence Agency doing at the home of the person who murdered Gao Hui and tried to kill us?" Moretti asked as he adjusted his scope and watched Tanner and Gillespie enter the foyer.

The alarm that sounded wasn't intrusive, nor did it bring Masterson's guards running. Instead, some might think it was a doorbell, although the mansion didn't have one. When they heard it, four guards calmly walked outside and joined the four who were getting into the two black Land Rover Defenders parked near the front entrance.

The thin man went to his office and looked at a display of perimeter cameras on his computer, focusing on the five individuals who were prone and trying to be unobtrusive in the mountainside snow. Although he couldn't own the land they were on because it was public, he nevertheless placed sensors there to warn him of intruders who might be surveilling his residence. Once a sensor was triggered, the cameras on the mansion's roof focused on that area, their resolution powerful enough to give the color of a person's eyes. Masterson recognized the intruders and returned to the foyer where Gillespie and Tanner were waiting.

"What do you know about the analysts who work for the White House?" he asked, not bothering to greet the US government employees or explain why he was asking.

"Only that they work for the president, and whatever they write is subject to executive privilege," Tanner answered.

"Meaning you don't know what they do."

"Not really."

Masterson filled them in on what happened to Moretti and Han Li while they were in transit to Davos and his belief that the White House Statistical Analysis Division was a group of operatives. "Moretti is an ex-Army Ranger, Bonaquist is ex-Secret Service, McGough is a former Force Recon Marine, Jian Shen is a Chinese national, and Han Li recently became a US citizen when she married Moretti," Masterson recited from memory, having excellent recall for details.

"Why is a Chinese national working in the White House?" Gillespie asked.

"A question I should ask one of you? However, the person I'm most concerned with, besides Cray, is Moretti. I'm familiar with him."

That statement surprised the two government employees.

"According to the photo accompanying the registration for the WEF, the name of the Asian we killed was Gao Hui, a member of China's Politburo Standing Committee. The person who survived the crash is General Chien An, the Chief of the General Staff of the PLA and a member of the Central Military Commission. He's the highest ranking military officer in China," Masterson said.

Gillespie and Tanner already knew their identities, using the government's database to identify the two senior Chinese officials, but they weren't going to rain on Masterson's parade by telling him.

"Have you considered the possibility that these White House analysts are covert operatives?"

"We haven't," Gillespie admitted.

"You should have. They'll be here shortly," Masterson said, explaining what he meant.

# ELEVEN

The Nemesis team didn't hear the Land Rover Defenders park behind their vehicles because the barrier of trees between them and the road muffled the noise. The eight security guards, familiar with the terrain, spread out and flanked the team, who was prone in the snow observing the mansion and didn't see the eight assault rifles pointed at them until it was too late. The guards disarmed the team, bound their hands with flex cuffs, and trudged them through the snow that encrusted the steep slope until they arrived at the Excursions. Three were placed in the back of one and two in the other, after which their ankles were cuffed.

The four vehicles departed with the Land Rovers in the lead and returned to the mansion, parking near the front entrance. Once their leg restraints were cut, the prisoners were escorted into the mansion and lined up in front of Masterson, Tanner, and Gillespie. As one of the guards spoke quietly to Masterson, the others stood behind the team with their assault rifles pointed at their backs. After their conversation, Masterson approached Moretti and Han Li, who were standing beside each other.

"I want to compliment you, Captain Moretti," Masterson said, referring to his military rank, "for being a formidable adversary. You may not know it, but we have a history. I'm the person who gave the order to destroy your Chinook helicopter in Afghanistan."

Moretti gave him a look of disbelief.

"It's true. Major Cray was going to Musa Qala to have the governor of Helmand Province sign a document that would have destroyed the provincial poppy fields producing half the world's opium. You and your Ranger team provided security for him."

The skepticism in Moretti's face faded.

"My family roots in Afghanistan run deep. We've been the sole buyer for that extract for generations, and I still am. It's made me a multi-billionaire and allowed me to purchase legitimate businesses. Therefore, you now understand why I couldn't allow that agreement to be signed and ordered the helicopter destroyed."

"And now, you want to kill all of us."

"You might interfere with my current plans."

"How could an analyst do that?"

"Let's eliminate the misnomer that you, Lieutenant Colonel Cray, or anyone else in that White House function is an analyst. The firearms my men found you carrying aren't tools that an analyst would use on the job. I believe you're here to investigate the Cabal and our new world order to determine the scope of our operations and find a way to stop us."

Moretti's body language, and the look of resignation on his face, indicated Masterson had hit the target.

"I will not let that happen. However, I respect your tenacity; therefore, I'm not averse to sharing our game plan because you and your team have earned the right to know it. Besides, I want to brag and tell you what you failed to stop."

"Aren't you going to introduce your friends?"

"Where are my manners? These are Adam Tanner, Deputy Director of the National Clandestine Service arm for the CIA, and Eugene Gillespie, Director of the military intelligence staff for the DIA. It goes without saying that since you've seen us, all of you will carry what I say to the grave."

"I saw their names and emails in one of Cray's reports, but I never saw a photo of them."

"I thought that you and your colleagues read those reports."

Moretti gave Masterson a look devoid of fear. "Establishing what some would call a new world order is nothing more than a dictatorship sheathed in a PR bubble where your accolades try to convince everyone that you're going to make their lives better, the planet greener, the politicians honest, and a package of other fantasies."

"Everyone's life will be better if they follow the rules."

"Your rules."

"Universal rules that sustain prosperity, order, and stability."

"For the ruling class."

Masterson smiled.

"How does this panacea start?" Moretti asked.

"It began more than a decade ago when we started promoting heterogenous borderless societies."

"Promoting is a fancy word for smuggling people from one nation to another."

"At the start. Once they tasted the good life and communicated this back home, the migration had a life of its own. It still does. Over time, nation-states will become ancestral artifacts. All humans occupy a single planet and should be free to choose where and in what society they want to live."

"How does that put you and your gang of misfits at the top of a new world order?"

Masterson ignored the insult and continued. "They'll eventually become voters. Until that happens, they influence political decision-making from the local to national level. Following this year's elections, we'll reach the tipping point for having the necessary global political influence."

"You'll never get most people to agree that a continuous and unrestrained invasion by uninvited outsiders is good for their nation and heritage. While they won't disagree with absorbing a reasonable number of foreigners into their citizenry, they're sure as hell not going to eliminate their borders—which is a wordy way of saying that nationalism will get in your way," Moretti replied.

"It will happen. We've spent tens of billions of dollars supporting migration, conducting intense political, social, and digital media campaigns, aligning the philosophies of major corporations to our agenda, and embedding the right to a borderless society in educational teachings. We have more than this amount in reserve to sustain these efforts and bring about the order.

"Set the migration aside. No one trusts politicians. Why would any country's citizenry give an outside group governance?"

"A democratic country gives governance to a select group every election. A dictator is replaced with another when he dies or when there's a coup. For most people, peace and prosperity are the defining factors for the acceptance of leadership. Change isn't relevant if you have a good life and a future; stability is important."

"It sounds good in theory, but the new world order is a delusional fantasy—a graduate paper, at best. It'll never happen."

"It's already started. The Republic of Cyprus and the Turkish Republic of Northern Cyprus have announced reunification talks because of their homogenous populations and the desire to eliminate the border between them. The People's Republic of China and the Republic of China, although that might be considered a shotgun wedding, will combine; Romania and Moldova; the UK, Canada, Australia, and New Zealand; the UK and Ireland; the Netherlands, Belgium, and Luxembourg; Russia will absorb Belarus and other fragments of the former Soviet Union; Bulgaria and Macedonia. I could go on and on. All they need is a push, which I'm giving them by funneling money into these countries to accelerate the process. However, even without the Cabal, many of these reunifications will still occur."

"And the Cabal meets here," Moretti stated, looking around the mansion's interior.

"Daily, during the forum. Social gatherings among attendees at the end of each day are the norm. That's when the business gets done. Therefore, our meeting of nearly a hundred members doesn't appear usual. If you were alive, you'd meet the heads of our committees and donors."

"If you have everything so well planned, why kill Cray and us?"

"I can't allow exposing what we're doing. This must appear to happen naturally. If it's known a group is behind global unification, many people won't accept it."

"A house of cards."

"Until we reach critical mass."

"You're a dictator with another storyline," Han Li said.

That comment seemed to hit Masterson's hot button. Nodding to the guard standing behind Han Li, he watched as he rammed his rifle into her back. That was an enormous mistake. In the blink of an eye, she turned and executed a karate kick the Japanese called yoko geri kekomi, or side thrust kick. It takes one thousand four hundred pounds of force to shatter a skull. Han Li's kick delivered twenty pounds more. The blow to the guard's temple crushed his skull, dropping him to the floor like a load of bricks. Masterson quickly raised his hand to stop the other guards from killing the martial arts expert because he still needed to interrogate her.

"Impressive," he said as he backed away, the seven remaining guards doing the same.

"If she moves, shoot her in the leg," Masterson said to the guards. "Getting back to why we're talking, I want to find out what all of you know about the Cabal."

Everyone remained silent.

"I can see this is going to take time," Masterson said, his voice a combination of disappointment and disgust. "Make no mistake that the process of getting you to answer my questions will be extremely painful. But, in the end, pain always loosens the tongue. Since I don't need all of you, let me illustrate your vulnerability," he said, pointing to McGough and telling the guard behind him to kill the Force Recon Marine. As he raised his rifle, Masterson suddenly raised his hand to stop the execution with a look of deep concern on his face. "You don't work at the White House," he said, looking at Chien An. "Where's the sixth member of your team?"

Jian Shen looked through his scope as the eight guards captured his teammates. The former PLA sniper, having been told by Moretti to cover the side of the house, was in an area outside that covered by the body heat monitoring devices planted in the mountain section facing the view windows. Although he was one of the best marksmen in the world, no one was fast enough to kill the eight men capturing his teammates before one sent a barrage of bullets in his direction. Without a vehicle, the Nemesis sniper had no choice but to stay out of sight and see if they took the team to the mansion, where the floor-to-ceiling windows provided him a view of what went on inside.

He saw the four-vehicle convoy drive through the enclave gates and his five teammates herded into the mansion after their leg restraints were cut. Besides the team and the eight guards escorting them, three others were visible inside—two sitting on the couch and Masterson standing in front of his prisoners talking. However, the appearance of calm was broken when one guard rammed his rifle into Han Li's back. Shen wasn't surprised by her response, nor the speed with which it was delivered. What did surprise him was that one of the other guards didn't shoot her—indicating Masterson wanted to keep at least some of the team alive.

Initially, when Shen set up his position on the mountain, he examined the glass windows through his scope, believing from their thickness and tint that they were bullet-resistant glass. He considered it illogical that someone would purchase this much land to guarantee their privacy, construct an enclaved mansion surrounded by high walls, have a security team, and then save a few bucks by installing traditional windows. Although the description commonly applied to these types of windows was bulletproof, he knew that was a myth, and they were only bullet-resistant—made by sandwiching between glass panes either a plastic acrylic or polycarbonate, which slowed down and absorbed the energy from a bullet. However, that didn't make it bulletproof.

Shen had an M107 sniper rifle and two magazines of .50 caliber armor-piercing rounds—which could penetrate level ten bullet-resistant glass, the highest protection rating given by a manufacturer. Even so, it would take incredible skill to hit a target on the other side of this glass barrier. For starters, a level ten plastic acrylic or polycarbonate glass would slow his round unpredictably and deflect the bullet as it penetrated the glass panes and plastic inserts. The farther a bullet was from perpendicular on impact, the greater this deflection. As a rule of thumb, this deviation ranged from 0.4 to 0.8 inches per foot beyond ordinary glass, and if it was bullet-resistant, that range increased. Collateral damage was also a concern because, as the bullet exited the glass, it carried a debris cloud containing thousands of fragments traveling at a similar velocity. This cloud expanded three and a half inches per foot for the first four feet. Lastly, as if hitting a target within the mansion couldn't get any more complicated, he needed to compensate for how much gravity would make the heavy bullet descend on its way to the target, along with the effects of wind and temperature.

Moving with practiced precision, he packed a mound of snow in front of him and placed the M107 on it to steady the gun and reduce the puff of snow that followed a muzzle blast. He then adjusted the scope for how much he expected the bullet would fall on its way to the target and its deflection. There was no compensation for the wind because the air was calm.

Focusing on the person closest to Moretti, for no other reason than he had to start somewhere, he steadied his breathing and relaxed his body. Even though shooting at someone was always stressful, getting rid of tension was vital because, at this long distance, the tiniest movement or muscle tenseness could make him miss, which is why he'd trained himself to shoot between heartbeats. Exhaling slowly, he stopped breathing, felt the rhythm of his heart, and ever so softly squeezed the trigger.

The .50 caliber bullet struck the guard in the back with fifteen thousand foot-pounds of force. The skeletal bone it hit and those beside it exploded into multiple shards, which flew throughout the body with the same force as a low-velocity bullet—instantly killing him. A second later, the person standing behind Han Li experienced similar back pain, followed by the person behind Chien An, whose chest exploded when he instinctively turned toward the window to look at the holes created by the armor-piercing rounds. After that—Masterson, Tanner, Gillespie, and the four surviving guards dove to the floor, not wanting to be the sniper's next victim.

With their hands bound behind their backs, the team bolted for the front door knowing that Shen was the shooter and would give them cover. One guard got up to try to stop them by reflex and was hit in the chest by another of Shen's rounds. After that, everyone in the room was catatonic and didn't move a muscle until well after they heard the cars at the front of the mansion race away.

Once outside, Bonaquist backed up to the door of an Excursion, opened it, and removed the knife he'd put in the glove compartment.

"Hold it firm," Moretti said as he backed up to the knife and sliced his ties on his second attempt, the first nicking the front of his wrist and drawing blood.

Taking it from Bonaquist, Moretti cut the bonds of the rest of the team, after which he took the wheel of one Excursion, with Han Li beside him. Bonaquist drove the other, with

McGough in the front and Chien An in the back. The vehicles then raced towards the gate—which automatically opened as they approached.

When they were captured, whatever they had on them was put into a white canvas bag, which was thrown on the floor of the front passenger seat of Moretti's Excursion. Han Li looked through the bag and dug out Moretti's phone. Handing it to him, she searched for hers as he called Shen and told him to get to the road.

Because going up the steep slope in knee-deep snow was significantly more demanding than going down, the two Excursions were waiting when Shen arrived and got into Moretti's vehicle. During that wait, Han Li distributed the bag's contents, and everyone discussed where they should regroup and plan their next move. All agreed that their hotel, and those around Davos, would be surveilled. Subsequently, they concluded their only safe haven was the American consulate in Zurich. They never made it.

# TWELVE

Masterson got off the floor, dusted himself off, and watched as four of his staff ran to their vehicles to try and recapture Moretti and his team. Given their adversaries' skills, he didn't expect that to happen. It wouldn't take long before they'd tell the president what he'd said in an arrogant display of stupidity. This made Tanner and Gillespie a liability since they could make a deal with the president to save their skins. Realizing he had no choice, he went to one of the fallen guards, picked up their assault rifle, and put a stream of bullets into them. Problem solved.

The thin man walked to one of a pair of white club chairs in the corner, which escaped the blood splatters, removed from the humidor between them a #1 Fuente Opus X cigar, which sold for one hundred fifty dollars, and lit it with his thirteen thousand dollar Dunhill Gold Apex lighter. Smoking calmed him down and sharpened his focus. Ten minutes later, he called the Albanian Mafia chieftain who orchestrated the snowplow assault. Their relationship was strictly business, and small talk was considered irrelevant and time-consuming.

"I have an urgent need for your services," Masterson said, explaining that five men and one woman left his Davos house in two black Ford Excursions, and he wanted them killed. He didn't explain the reason because that was also irrelevant.

"How long ago did they leave?"

Masterson told him.

"The cost is double my usual contract price."

"What are you waiting for?"

Before getting onto the highway, the team rearmed themselves to the teeth with weapons from the rear of the vehicles. There were two routes from Davos to Zurich. One was to take rural roads, which meandered through the mountains and were only cleared of snow after the main highway was pristine. The other was to take highway twenty-eight. Moretti chose this route because it was the fastest, and although it was clear, the recent clearing left a glistening six feet high pile of snow along its edge. He and Bonaquist had their pedal to the metal, traveling at eighty mph, which was twenty over the expressway limit. Everything was going well until they approached the town of Bad Ragaz, which was forty-four minutes from Davos, where they stopped behind a line of cars, watching as the vehicles at the front made a U-turn.

"Let me find out what's going on," Moretti said to Han Li as he pulled the Excursion to the side of the road and got out. Bonaquist did the same and accompanied him. Walking to the head of the line, they saw a snowdrift blocked the road a hundred yards behind a barrier across the highway. They came back and told the rest of the team.

"They'll probably use that beast to open the highway," Han Li said, pointing to the massive dump truck with a thirty-two-foot blade on the other side of the road.

"That'll do the job. Back to Davos or wait for the beast to clear the highway?" Shen asked.

"We don't know when they'll start or how long it will take. Let's take the scenic route," Moretti said, asking Han Li to get a road map of the area on her phone and see how they could get on the rural road.

As Moretti spoke to Han Li, the two snowplow operators were looking at the occupants of both Excursions.

"That's them," the driver said, referencing the photos on his cellphone.

The plan formulated by the Albanian Mafia chieftain was for them to block highway twenty-eight by taking the snow from either side and spreading it across the thoroughfare. As traffic stopped, they were to look for two black Ford Excursions carrying the people in the texted photos. Ten minutes after they began watching the line of cars making U-turns in front of the barrier they erected, the two Excursions came to a stop. They watched as two occupants got out, looked at the pile of snow across the highway, and returned to their vehicles. Wanting to kill everyone at once, they waited for their return.

"Let's get this done," the driver said, putting the giant truck in gear.

Their plan was for the plow to hit the two vehicles broadside, with the blade tearing through both Excursions and the truck finishing the job by crushing what was left. Since the truck weighed fifty-eight thousand seven hundred forty pounds, and the plow added another nine thousand, no one was going to survive the aftermath of that collision.

The massive snowplow wasn't nimble and couldn't accelerate any faster than a bill going through the US Congress. It also wasn't quiet, the huge diesel engine so noisy that it could be heard for a mile or more as it billowed black exhaust into the clear mountain air. Therefore, when it started, the Nemesis team turned toward the erupting sound and saw the enormous machine coming toward them. Seeing there wasn't any snow between the plow and the Excursions, and the driver was alternating looking intently at Moretti and Bonaquist, no one doubted the plow was coming for them.

Usually, getting out of its way wouldn't be difficult because the difference between the Excursion and the snowplow's acceleration and turning radiuses were night and day. However, the person behind Bonaquist's vehicle was only a few inches from it, approximately the same number of inches he was behind the other Excursion. To compound the problem, the car in front of Moretti decided to back up to get enough room to make a U-turn, meaning he had no room in front of him. It was the perfect storm.

"Grab your weapons and get out of the car," Moretti ordered Han Li and Shen. The same command Bonaquist gave when he saw what was happening.

The giant truck accelerated to five mph from a standstill and worked its way to ten as the driver deftly moved through its gears. Since the distance between the truck and the Excursions was sixty-five feet, the team had six seconds to get out of the vehicles before being flattened. Everyone was out in four except for Shen, who was trying to manipulate his fifty-seven-inch long M107 rifle within the confines of the car to get a shot at the plow driver. Getting the nearly five feet long, thirty-pound weapon into firing position took slightly less than two seconds, which meant the colossal snowplow blade was inches from the vehicle when he raised it.

The Albanian Mafioso in the passenger seat saw the team escape from the Excursions and knew the plow wouldn't get the job done. Grabbing the automatic rifle off the floorboard, he switched the selector to full auto, meaning his weapon would fire fifteen rounds per second from the thirty bullet magazine, and set his sights on Bonaquist, who was furthest to the left. He intended to sweep the weapon to the right, killing everyone before they knew what had happened. That plan might have worked had Shen not seen the Albanian stick the barrel of his automatic weapon out the passenger window and put an armor piercing round into his forehead. However, with no time to turn the heavy gun on the driver, he dropped it and bolted for the side passenger door, getting there as the four-and-a-half-ton blade sliced through the spot in the vehicle where he'd been a moment earlier. However, because the tremendous weight of the blade bent the frame,

Shen couldn't open the door. With the windows shattered and the vehicle half its size, he saw the heavy plow blade continuing to come toward him. Hearing a gunshot in the distance, the last thing he remembered seeing before his head slammed into the shrinking vehicle's roof was the manufacturer's stenciled name on the blade.

It took an hour for a rescue team to arrive. Using the hydraulic extraction tool called the jaws of life, the operator inserted its spreader. This pincer-like arm applied fourteen thousand four hundred pounds of pulling force into one of the openings torn in the vehicle and expanded the hole. Afterward, he used the tool's cutter—a big chomper that bit through the metal, to widen the hole and expose the vehicle's interior.

While the paramedics were attempting to get to Shen, the police had questions for the Nemesis team, including explaining why they killed the snowplow operator and his assistant, both Swiss citizens—one shot by Shen and the other by Moretti. The extensive weaponry in their vehicles' trunks was of less concern because Swiss laws on the possession of firearms were among the most liberal in the world, permitting ownership of even fully automatic weapons by citizens and foreigners within or outside their residence. With laws focusing on the acquisition of firearms, not their ownership, and the diplomatic plates on the Excursions, the police didn't want to touch the issue of weapons.

When the police interviewed witnesses, they learned the snowplow operator intentionally drove the blade on his truck into the two stationary vehicles while his passenger aimed the automatic rifle found in it at the Excursions. With both men in the truck dead, and upon hearing these accounts, the police decided to throw the incident in the lap of the Federal Department of Foreign Affairs.

Because Shen's Excursion was a twisted maze of steel, the paramedics didn't get to him for twenty minutes. Once they found he was alive, a medical tech entered the vehicle and, while his partner passed him supplies, hooked Shen to an IV and took his vitals.

"How is he?" Moretti asked the tech's partner.

"He's conscious and not in critical condition. But we won't know the extent of his injuries until he gets to the hospital."

That Shen was alive and conscious eased the team's tension. Fifteen minutes later, he was lifted from the vehicle and gave a thumbs up to the team as the paramedics put him on a gurney.

"Han Li and I will go with him in the ambulance," Moretti said.

"What about our weapons?" McGough asked. "I'm not sure the Swiss will let us carry them around."

"Let me ask one of the officers," Moretti said, returning several minutes later and telling him that the police volunteered to hold their weapons at their station in Davos.

"And the handguns?"

"What handguns?" Moretti asked, knowing that every member hid them in the small of their backs and under their clothing before the police arrived.

Tenant Masterson should have been angry when the Mafia chieftain phoned and told him that everyone survived the attack and they were on their way to the Spital Davos Hospital, accompanying one of their team who had non-life-threatening injuries. He'd come to terms that he was facing seasoned operatives whose skills exceeded those of his men and the contract killers he sometimes employed. Because of this, he had only one option: to expose that the president of the United States had an assassination squad and was hiding them under the guise of being White House analysts. To propagate this, he called for his social media genius. On cue, Kimmel entered the room and explained what had happened and what he wanted.

In the chair beside Masterson, Kimmel took a cigar from the humidor and joined the reclusive leader of the Cabal, who was puffing on his #1 Fuente Opus X. "The president will deny the accusations and ask for proof. Without it, the country won't unite against him."

"What do you suggest?"

"If you repeat a lie often enough, even if it's a lie, it will eventually become the truth."

"A policy of the Nazi Joseph Goebbels."

"Over three-quarters of a century later, it's still true. I'll have several teams repeat this accusation about the president's analysts until it's accepted as truth, banning anyone with a countervailing point of view from my sites. But accusations are not proof."

"What is?"

"They have law enforcement and military backgrounds. If we check, I'm sure we'll discover they haven't taken one statistics or analytics course between them. How can they be analysts, especially at the level of the White House, if they don't have that skills? That's proof this division is a scam."

"Genius, which is why you're my vice-chair."

Shen was released from the hospital the following morning, having suffered a minor concussion and a multitude of cuts and abrasions. The police returned them to the Tschuggen Grand Hotel in Arosa, providing 24/7 protection at the direction of the Federal Department of Foreign Affairs, who didn't want to get on the wrong side of President Ballinger by having anyone associated with the White House assaulted or killed. While Nemesis knew this protection would keep Masterson's men away, they also realized it ended their surveillance efforts. They were discussing how to get around this limitation at a table in the lobby when Moretti received a call from Vice-President Houck. When he finished, he put his phone on the table.

"We're busted," he said. "Social media is blowing up with allegations that S-A-D is the president's assassination squad."

"Masterson," Bonaquist said.

"The FBI will reissue the warrants for Han Li and me—the president accused of previously quashing them for political gain. With Congress calling for hearings, this effectively deactivates Nemesis and may get the president impeached," Moretti said.

"They'll accuse him of obstruction of justice for quashing the warrants, and every Congressperson wanting to be on the evening news and get their fifteen minutes of fame will call for his impeachment."

"The day after tomorrow, at eight in the evening, the consulate will have a car to take us to the Aviano Air Base in Italy, which is a six-hour drive, and a military aircraft will take us back to the states. When we land in DC, it'll be six in the morning local time, and we'll go straight to the White House. We're going military because the vice-president said it would be a feeding frenzy at the departing and arriving airports if we'd taken a commercial flight. He's delaying our departure a couple of days to try and let things cool down and speak with the president's advisors, the DOJ, members of Congress, and so forth to discuss how they should handle things when we arrive."

Everyone had differing opinions on what would happen when they returned to DC. However, they all agreed with Moretti's previous assumption that this ended Nemesis, President Ballinger's presidency, and Vice-President Houck's term of office since it would come out that he worked closely with the team. This meant the Speaker of the House, from the same political party as the president, would become the new leader of the free world after their impeachments. Moretti knew the Speaker and felt he was a space cadet who couldn't open a refrigerator door without a set of instructions.

"Because Han Li works for the president, and I'm here with you," Chien An said, "it'll eventually come out that President Ballinger is working with President Liu. With that revelation, the Communist Party will call for a National People's Congress meeting to elect a new president."

"And there's nothing we can do to stop it," McGough said with a note of resignation.

Seeing Moretti seemingly lost in thought, Han Li asked what he was thinking.

"That we turn the tables on Masterson."

# THIRTEEN

Moretti's plan required them to leave the hotel unnoticed, which wouldn't be easy because of their police protective detail, one of whom was standing next to the doorway while their partner was in a patrol car outside. They were returning to the area where they previously observed Masterson's residence, staying on the road to avoid the sensors he'd placed on the slope where they viewed the mansion.

Chien An solved the transportation problem, noticing that two vans with the hotel's name stenciled on their sides were only visible from behind the hotel. Therefore, neither officer would see them getting into one of them. However, they needed to drive past the patrol car to get to the road.

Sunset in Davos occurred at six thirty-seven p.m. Bonaquist opened the hotel's backdoor at five, giving the team an hour and a half of daylight to execute his plan. Standing six feet eight inches tall, he extended his arms and pulled the electrical cable to the security camera above it that looked onto the rear parking area. Having discussed this earlier, no one was surprised that one of the hotel staff didn't come outside to check why the video was down. They believed the hotel's camera system was used for deterrence and documentation, and management wouldn't waste money having someone stare at a computer screen 24/7. That assumption was correct.

McGough was the first to arrive at a van and, using a coat hanger from his room, bent it into a jimmy and opened its door. Using the screwdriver attachment on his pocketknife, he removed the screws on both sides of the steering column and the cover. There were three bundles of wires beneath, each a different color. He knew from training that the ignition wire was usually black and the battery wire red. Using his knife, he cut these wires, stripped the insulation off the ends, and twisted them together. Next, he cut the starter motor wire and touched it to the other two. The engine started.

The drive to the road carved into the mountain facing Masterson's mansion took twenty-five minutes, Moretti telling McGough to stop the vehicle when it was beside a rectangular structure on twenty feet high heavy steel pilings with a garage door-sized opening on one side. He'd previously seen the unmarked aluminum building, a quarter mile from where the team parked the Excursions when surveilling the mansion, and knew what was inside.

Chien An was the first one up the ladder that led to the entry door, telling those below he couldn't get inside because an Abus stainless steel lock secured the sliding latch.

"Since we don't have lock-picking tools, any ideas on the best way to get inside?" Moretti asked.

McGough, who was at the bottom of the ladder, didn't answer. Instead, he went to the van, returning a few minutes later with the tire jack handle, which he wedged between the lock and the sliding latch. The three hundred five pounds former Marine had done his share of breaching in Force Recon and ripped the latch off on his third tug. The first to enter the structure, he pulled the handle on a steel box beside the door, which activated a series of high-intensity lights overhead. To their left was an M101A1 105 mm howitzer. The four thousand nine hundred eighty pound artillery piece was nineteen feet six inches long, seven feet three inches wide, five feet eight inches high, and had a barrel length of slightly under eight feet. The range of the thirty-six-pound ten-ounce shell it fired was twelve thousand three hundred thirty yards.

"Explain how you knew this would be in the building?" Bonaquist asked, amazed that Moretti was right about the weapon.

"I grew up in Alaska and spent four winters working for ski resorts that used artillery shells to prevent unexpected avalanches."

"I didn't know that resorts had one of these?" Shen asked.

"Not everyone does. There are two primary ways to trigger a small avalanche before it develops into one that's large. The first is to use a Gazex cannon. It's not a traditional cannon, such as this howitzer. Instead, it's a large pipe that faces downward. Propane and oxygen ignite in a chamber and emit hot gases. The explosive burst causes a small avalanche which disperses accumulated snow. The howitzer does the same thing, but in my experience, it can take as many as fifteen shells for the avalanche to start."

"I'm curious; what's a large avalanche?" McGough asked.

"A million tons of snow traveling two hundred mph."

Those numbers surprised the team.

Moretti turned to Chien An. "Did you ever fire a howitzer?" Knowing he wasn't a field artillery officer, he didn't bother to ask the Force Recon Marine.

"It's identical to our 105 mm SH2 and SH5 cannons," the Chinese general answered.

"How do we get started?"

"We look for the propellant charge, projectiles, and detonators."

"There's only one place they could be," Moretti responded, looking at two locked steel containers at the rear of the structure.

McGough didn't need an invitation and used the car jack handle to break into each.

"These are the projectiles," Chien An said after looking inside one container. "We call that the wine rack because they're stored horizontally like wine bottles."

"They don't look like any artillery shells I've seen," McGough commented, seeing the thirty-five pound, three feet long rounds.

"That's because they're unarmed," he said before going to the other container and identifying its contents as the detonators and propellant charges.

As Chien An began preparing the shells, Moretti opened the folding steel door in front of the howitzer; the cannon pointed at a mountain slope forty degrees to the right of Masterson's home.

"How many shells will we need?" Chien An asked.

"I don't know. It depends on the stability of the snowpack. As I said, I've fired as many as fifteen. Because the sun doesn't shine on that area of the mountain, there's not much fluctuation in temperature, which would produce intermittent melting and instability. The slope isn't particularly steep, and there's no snowboarding or snowmobiling, which would put pressure on the snowpack. Therefore, my guess is that the snow on the slope behind the mansion is very stable. Masterson wouldn't have built his residence there otherwise. That means it'll take some effort to create instability in an inherently stable snowpack. To answer your question, prep all the shells because, once we start, we won't have time to stop and put together another batch. When Masterson catches on to what we're doing, he and the other Cabal members will leave the mansion. We may never get another chance like this.

"How do you know the avalanche will be large enough to destroy the house?" Bonaquist asked.

"Judging from the mountain slope, we're looking at a thousand to ten thousand tons of snow and debris. Anything in that range will crush and bury the house." Turning to Chien An he said: "We'll aim for a spot twenty yards from the top of the slope and work our way to the left and right of the initial impact point." The general nodded in agreement.

It took Chien An fifteen minutes to finish inserting the detonators and readying the shells. While he was doing this, the rest of the team moved the heavy weapon to point it at the slope behind the residence, although they had no idea what the barrel's elevation should be. Chien An solved that problem by referencing a chart on the side of the weapon, which gave the elevation for a given distance and outside temperature. Although both were guesstimates, he'd gone through this procedure multiple times on the S2 and S5 systems and knew that he would put the shells within a gnat's whisker of its target.

The first shell, and ten subsequent rounds, landed on target. An experienced artillery team can fire six M101A1 105 mm howitzer rounds per minute. The Nemesis team managed two, the eleven rounds taking six minutes to pummel the mountain slope and loosen the snowpack. Upon reaching its tipping point, the disintegrating snowpack became an avalanche carrying one hundred thousand tons of snow and ice down the mountain at two hundred mph. Within seconds, the enormous mansion was torn apart and buried under a white blanket of snow.

"It's hard to believe anyone could have survived," McGough stated.

"They'll be air pockets under the snow and ice, but hypothermia and diminishing air will make survival difficult unless rescue teams get here shortly," Moretti responded.

"It looks like the mansion had an escape tunnel," Han Li said, pointing to two persons who opened a hatch two hundred fifty yards from where the residence stood.

"I can't see their faces from this distance, but one looks rail thin, even in a parka. We need to capture him—alive if possible. If they went to the expense of building an escape tunnel, they'd have a vehicle near the exit. We need to catch them before they get to it," Moretti said as he closed the folding steel door in front of the cannon and followed the team down the ladder, McGough taking the tire jack with him.

Getting in the van, they went down the road toward the escape hatch, the road meandering as it descended, eventually intersecting another road. Several hundred yards away, they saw two black Mercedes G-class SUVs exiting a barn and going in opposite directions. Each had darkened windows, making it impossible to see inside. Moretti focused on the vehicle coming towards them and blocked the road, giving the driver two choices—hit the van or go around it. Because the G-wagon is excellent at going through snow, the driver took the second option. That would have been a sound decision had it not been for the large rocks hidden beneath it.

A Mercedes G-wagon requires nine and a half inches of ground clearance. The height of the rocks beneath the snow at the side of the road started at ten and went up from there. With a fractured housing and a broken driveshaft, the G-wagon came to an abrupt stop. Seeing the vehicle was stuck, the Nemesis team ran to it; Han Li arrived first, kicked in the driver's side window, and grabbed Peter Kimmel, pulling him out of the car and onto the snow.

"Put him in the van and let's get out of here before someone sees us," Moretti said.

Kimmel had no intention of going quietly. He'd taken years of private lessons in several martial arts and believed he was a badass. Given a sixth-degree black belt by his three instructors, who stroked his Silicon Valley narcissism and let him beat up on them so they could continue to be on his company's payroll, Kimmel decided to showcase his skills and confront the only woman on the team. He believed that easily defeating her would strike fear in the others, and he'd subdue them without a fight. He screamed his kiai, the shout uttered before performing an attacking move, and came at her.

Han Li didn't have a martial arts belt. Before Nemesis, she employed her skills in life and death situations where the loser was put in a body bag regardless of the belt they wore. Formerly China's top assassin, she was groomed from early childhood for a career as an off-the-books asset of the Second Bureau, which conducted operations abroad. If she ever stepped into a martial arts class, she would have been considered a twelfth-degree black belt in karate, taekwondo, and krav maga.

The average person will punch at a speed of fifteen mph, and the average boxer at twenty-five. One has exceptional speed if they can throw a punch at around thirty-two mph, and those with extraordinary skills at forty-five mph or higher. Han Li's was forty-eight. Kimmel decided to go for an immediate knockout and throw an oi-zuki, or lunging punch, the most powerful in karate, where the person steps forward and puts his body weight behind a thrust that travels in a straight line. The Silicon Valley narcissist practiced this on his instructors and never failed to put them on the ground grimacing in pain. With a punch clocked by one of them at twenty-four mph, he expected Han Li to be much slower. However, with twice his "clocked" speed, she raised her blocking arm and met his strike, deftly bending her elbow forty-five degrees and lifting her arm in an arc that redirected his blow to the side and over her head. Kimmel, off balance because he put everything he had into his punch and struck nothing but air, leaned forward to regain his footing. He never did, Han Li planting a fist in his solar plexus with such force that he dropped to the ground gasping for air.

"Put Bruce Lee into the van," Moretti said to McGough and Shen, who were standing beside each other. Once everyone was inside, Moretti and Han Li in the back kneeling on either side of Kimmel, he told Bonaquist to drive.

"Where should we take him?" Bonaquist shouted into the back of the van before putting it in gear.

"The hotel. We need to return this vehicle, and I have something I want to discuss with him."

Bonaquist turned the van around.

"Do you know who I am?" Kimmel asked Moretti, his arrogance on par with that of Masterson.

"You're the major shareholder of one of the largest social media companies in the world."

"Then you know I have enough influence to orchestrate whatever I want to happen to you, the president, or anyone else on this planet. Let's negotiate. What do you want?"

"I want you to unwrap what you've done to the president and us and discredit that story as fake news. Next, you will ensure his political enemies don't have a voice in countering that argument. Lastly, you're dropping your support of the Cabal and blocking the accounts of every member."

"That's not going to happen. Even if you kill me, another Cabal member in my company will ensure our views prevail."

"The Cabal's leadership is under a pile of snow."

"Masterson and over seventy-five percent of it isn't. You don't get it. Everyone on this planet is a worker bee except for us. We're too powerful for anyone, even a nation-state, to defeat or minimize. You can't stop the Cabal or the new world order. You're a surfer trying to paddle through a tsunami. I can make a reasonable deal to keep all of you out of jail, but the president and vice-president must be impeached."

"I'm not here to negotiate. I ask questions, and you answer. Where's Masterson?"

"I'm not going to say, and there's nothing you can do to make me change my mind."

"I think there is."

# FOURTEEN

They pulled the van into the rear of the hotel at six-thirty that evening with Kimmel still shouting that he would have them all thrown in jail.

"We can't bring him into the hotel like this," Moretti said to Han Li. "He needs to be sedated."

Taking the hint, Han Li put him in a chokehold, interfering with the blood flow from the carotid artery to the brain and inducing unconscious. McGough then threw him over his shoulders and went into the building. Once everyone was inside, Bonaquist reconnected the electrical cable to the surveillance camera and followed the team to Moretti's room.

"Put him on the bed and tie and gag him," Moretti said to McGough.

"Was that bravado, or do you have a way for Kimmel to unwrap what he's said about the president, vice-president, and us?" Bonaquist asked.

"I was serious."

"How?"

"By having him reverse what he said."

"He's an egomaniacal narcissist. He'd rather give up his laptop than lose face with his millions of followers."

"He'll do it."

"If he steam-rolled the president, who could make him reverse his statements?" Bonaquist questioned.

"Libby Parra."

A howitzer discharging a round produces a one hundred eighty-one decibel sound—more than the one hundred fifty decibels from a commercial jet engine at full power on takeoff. Therefore, the cannon blasts could be heard at a minimum of ten miles and possibly as far as fifty, depending on atmospheric conditions and the attenuation produced by the wooded mountain slopes. Their hotel in Arosa was seven and a half miles away as the crow flew, which meant everyone in town heard and knew the cause of the blast. As the cannon had been discharging shells into the surrounding mountains for over three decades, no one thought the firings were unusual. The police had the same opinion and, even though they were usually notified before it was fired, there were times when that notification fell through the cracks.

Since Masterson's mansion had no neighbors within sight of the residence, no one was aware of the avalanche until the following morning when a driver on the mountain road on which the howitzer structure sat thought it odd that he couldn't see a sliver of the mansion that was always visible through the trees. Stopping his car, he slowly walked down the steep slope until he saw a pile of snow in place of the mansion.

The sixty-three-year-old life-long Davos resident was an easy forty pounds overweight and believed he got enough exercise lifting a beer stein, which weighed five pounds when filled with Hopfenperle, his favorite brew. Therefore, as he walked back up the slope with the rapid increase in adrenaline flowing into his body due to what he saw, his heart rate and blood pressure shot off the scale. Because excess adrenaline narrowed the small arteries to the heart, it temporarily decreased the blood flow. As a result, when the elderly man stepped onto the roadway, short of breath and sweating profusely, his heart finally threw in the towel and stopped beating.

His body was discovered an hour later by a motorist, who phoned the police. A squad car with two officers arrived a short time later, quickly determining the beer meister was dead. Following internal procedures, one of the officers requested a detective along with the coroner and medical examiner.

While one officer cordoned off the area around the deceased and his vehicle, the other followed his footsteps in the snow and descended the slope, eventually seeing that a massive mound of snow had replaced the mansion, a residence with which he and those who lived in the area were familiar. He called it in.

Since everyone who lived within a radius of ten-plus miles, which included the two officers, heard the howitzer, it didn't take much imagination to believe the snow cannon caused the avalanche. The officer returned to his vehicle and told his partner what he'd seen. Both agreed they should look at the cannon.

Once those who'd been dispatched arrived at the scene, they drove there. From their car, they could see that the entry door was open. Climbing the ladder, they inspected the building and saw the latch on the door, and those on the storage containers, were ripped off. Treating the building as a crime scene, one officer returned to their vehicle, removed a roll of yellow crime scene tape from the trunk, and placed several strips across the door, after which they called the station and told the dispatcher what they'd discovered.

The Swiss share the German and Austrian propensities for having checklists and procedures for almost any anticipated event. In this instance, the Canton police had a checklist detailing what to do if there was a break-in of the building containing the howitzer. The first item was to call the duty officer at the SLF, or Institute for Snow and Avalanche Research, which had operational responsibility for the cannon.

The SLF official who was unfortunate enough to be on call wasn't in the best of moods. He was unhappy at having to leave his family on the ski slopes to inspect a break-in at an avalanche prevention tool he considered a relic. The SLF had long advocated to the Canton that the Gazex system replace the howitzer. However, they ignored these requests because of the one hundred fifty thousand dollar price tag. Since the howitzer was on loan to the town from the government because it was surplus equipment, the only cost was the three hundred dollar shells.

The official showed his creds to the officer at the bottom of the ladder and followed him through the entry door, where the first thing he noticed was that the containers were open and that cannon shells were missing. His eyes immediately went to the howitzer, seeing that someone had turned it.

"Did you move the cannon?" he asked the officer, receiving a negative response and a look that questioned if the official had a full deck of cards because of the weapon's size.

The official ignored the look and raised the folding steel door. Stepping in front of the howitzer, he saw it was aimed at the top of the mountain with the most stable snowpack in the area; only the snow was gone. He went to the container with the missing shells and started counting.

"What should I report?" the officer asked.

"Someone fired eleven rounds into the mountain to start the avalanche. Given the changes in the cannon's direction and elevation needed to hit the upper slope, whoever fired the howitzer was skilled in its use."

"The detectives will ask for a list of employees certified to fire this gun?"

The official said he had that list and would provide it when requested.

As this was occurring, a detachment of police and ski patrol rescue workers arrived at the mansion, beginning the task of looking for survivors. Most believed they were there to retrieve bodies. The reason for this bleak assessment were government statistics that showed a ninety-two percent chance of survival if someone was rescued within fifteen minutes of an avalanche, decreasing to thirty-seven percent after thirty-five minutes.

When the avalanche rescue team arrived, they first checked for a signal from a RECCO rescue system, the passive reflector device unobtrusively sewn into many ski garments. However, no signal was detected. As this occurred, two dogs trained to find avalanche victims began sniffing the massive mound of snow. Because a dog's sense of smell is thousands of times better than humans and can detect the sweat of those buried in the snow, they found victim after victim. The rescuers soon realized that many people were still buried beneath them and that they needed heavy equipment to remove the mansion's debris to get to them. Because of the size of the structure and the amount of snow, that removal took some time.

Libby Parra was a forty-eight-year-old statuesque blonde. Considered the top analyst at the Agency, her reports routinely ended up on the desk of the president and other top government officials. Ten years past the date she could have retired, she told the current director that she was committed to working there until dropping at her desk. When asked why Parra said she made America safer. He agreed.

Her last contact with the Nemesis team was months ago when she'd helped them find the terrorists who stole two nuclear weapons before they could detonate them in Shanghai and Beijing. During that episode, she'd worked with Cray but knew Moretti, who was now calling her encrypted cellphone.

"You and your team have become infamous on social media," Parra said without preface.

"I've heard."

"Several members of Congress, all of whom have, in my opinion, the intelligence of a snail darter, have expressed their intent to get you and your team in front of their committees so they can get their faces on the major news networks and splashed across the world. They want to take you, the president, and vice-president down for political gain."

"That's why I'm calling. Have you heard of the Cabal?"

"Why are you asking?"

Moretti took fifteen minutes explaining everything that happened, including what he knew about Masterson, his introduction to Tanner and Gillespie, and the kidnapping of Kimmel.

"You've been busy. Are you sure it was Tanner and Gillespie?"

"Masterson introduced them."

There was a moment of silence before Parra continued. "Let's put aside whether the NSA is aware of the Cabal. What do you want?"

"If their members communicated, I assume the NSA recorded those conversations. If those show, as I believe, that the president, vice-president, and Nemesis were set up, I can convince Kimmel to unwarp what he's done."

"There's a lot of ifs in those assumptions."

"I know. But I need to show that Kimmel is part of the Cabal and shaping public opinion to discredit the administration and us to establish a new world order. If I can't, we'll all be tattooed by this elitist scumbag. With the government in turmoil and Kimmel's control of social media, the public will be led to believe that their best way forward is a new world order. Those with dissenting points of view won't be digitally heard and will need snail mail to contact voters and offer a contrarian opinion."

Although Moretti didn't know it, protecting the United States was Parra's hot button, and Moretti struck a nerve. "I'll call you back shortly," she said, ending the call.

When Moretti mentioned Gillespie and Tanner's names, she immediately knew why their conversations hadn't come to her attention and bypassed the Agency's robust algorithms that should have flagged them. She started digging.

The first step in that process was to access the NSA's central data repository in Bluffdale, Utah. Referred to as the UDC, the two billion dollars, one million square feet facility was designed to store yottabytes of data—a yottabyte is a septillion bytes or five hundred quintillions (500,000,000,000,000,000,000) pages of text. She wanted conversations that occurred using the classified series of frequencies and access protocols to one of its communications satellites, which Tanner and Gillespie could access. If what she suspected was true, they gave these protocols and passwords to Cabal members enabling them to modify their satphones to communicate over these frequencies.

It took less than a minute to get a list of unauthorized persons who used the NSA frequencies and retrieve their voice and electronic communications. She discovered four hundred eighty-three Cabal members, many of whom resided in foreign countries. Because the NSA allowed only a few members to access their satellite, she called Moretti.

"I have what you want," Parra said without preface. "Put Kimmel on the phone."

Moretti didn't know what she would tell the media mogul, but from the sound of her voice, it wasn't going to be something he would like. He ungagged the social media guru and gave him his phone. With his hands bound and in front of him, Kimmel lifted it to his left ear.

When Parra identified herself, the narcissistic media mogul began threatening her and the Agency, indicating that everyone involved in what happened to him would be in jail while he was sucking up rays on his five hundred and three feet long superyacht. Parra was quiet during this tirade and, when he finished, cleared her throat.

"Let me give you a dose of reality," she said. "I have recordings of your conversations with members of the Cabal that prove you've violated the Foreign Agent Registration Act or FARA. In case you're too lame to know what that means—you acted in the interests of another government without filing the necessary disclosure documents. The evidence will show that the group you collude with, the Cabal, is spending billions to influence national and local legislation, elections, trade, and other issues with international ramifications. At the same time, your media company actively excludes contrarian viewpoints. These are clear violations of FARA."

"You're fishing. We have a two thousand forty-eight bit digital key in our satphones, and my techs tell me it would take three hundred trillion years to crack communications protected by this key."

"Unless one has a quantum computer. We decrypted your conversations in ten seconds."

"Bullshit. I'm not blinking. We're at least five to ten years away from that technology. I should know because my company is the first in line to receive those computers once they're manufactured."

"The NSA has a policy of inventing and engineering for capabilities that others won't realize for a decade or more. Let me prove it to you." Parra read a conversation Kimmel had with a member of the German government.

The media mogul was silent for a moment, then came at Parra with what he believed was his ace in the hole. "Section 230 of Title 47 of the US Code gives me and my company immunity from liability for third-party content, indicating we're neither a publisher nor speaker. Anyone can say anything they want on social media. It's called freedom of speech."

"Freedom of speech isn't the issue, and we're not talking third-party. You still must register as a foreign agent. Also, you used NSA satellites without our permission when acting as a foreign agent. You also moved a great deal of money that I'm sure you didn't disclose in your tax filings. You may be one of the world's largest social media companies, but the president has the bully pulpit. When he gives a press conference and starts reading some of your conversations, you'll be radioactive to every politician and lobbyist in the world. The Department of Justice will also want to speak with you, either before or after your indicted."

"What do you propose?" Kimmel asked in a manner that indicated he was open to accepting whatever Parra offered.

"The inferences on the White House Statistical Analysis Division and those who work there, along with what was said about the president and vice-president, must be walked back. You'll say that after an extensive investigation, you concluded that your company was duped, published erroneous information, and apologizes for what occurred. You will defend those statements, no matter what."

"We're not a publisher."

"Right. Tell that to someone who believes that bullshit. You will not mention what happened to you. If you do, the analysts you're with will pay you a visit. You won't survive."

"You're threatening me."

"Absolutely."

"That's it?"

"Not quite. You may get a call from me from time to time asking you to discredit a post, suspend, or ban someone from your site. In this way, I'll be sure you don't use a surrogate to make innuendos that I find unhelpful."

"And in return, I'm not charged with a crime now or in the future, and I won't ever see these analysts again."

"That's the deal."

"What about if I'm called by another member of the Cabal? That's going to happen."

"Not for long."

# FIFTEEN

The retraction by the social media giant ended the calls for impeachment and Congressional investigations. It also rescinded the newly issued warrants for the arrests of Moretti and Han Li. Instead, there was a backlash in Congress where both parties discussed repealing Section 230 and creating better oversight over media giants to ensure something like this couldn't occur again. In addition, the White House gave Congressional committees a stack of classified analytical reports produced by Alexson and Connelly to stem the flow of questions about the competency of his analysts. That these were meaningful reports not seen by any of the alphabet agencies or the DOD, and the president didn't exert executive privilege to prevent their disclosure, went a long way to disprove the allegations against the team. Within a week, politicians focused on something new they could turn into a crisis to get their names in the media and help raise funds.

The NSA changed the frequencies to its satellite and gave them to a smaller group, which could only access it using a satphone issued by the NSA. The chips and printed circuit boards within these phones were unduplicatable. A tamper-proof coating prevented x-ray examination and was so dense that it couldn't be picked away and its PCB tracks traced. Resistors and capacitors used on the PCB displayed the wrong values, so anyone who got through the coating would read the deceptive values atop the components. Finally, hidden micro-bond wires ran over the chips and tamper-proof coating. If someone attempted to grind the coating layer off, they'd cut the nearly invisible ten-micron wires.

The NSA passed the list of the Cabal members who hadn't perished in the avalanche to its intelligence counterparts in countries where that organization operated. Most were arrested and charged with whatever laws the government determined they violated. Some weren't prosecuted because law enforcement either felt there wasn't enough evidence to bring against them in a court of law, or the revelation of what occurred made the government appear as if they were asleep at the switch.

President Ballinger had one of these dilemmas with Samuel Bradford and Desmond Pruitt, who escaped prosecution because of a sleight of hand by Masterson. Suspecting the walls were closing in on him, he sent a message to Kimmel that the two undisclosed members who used Bradford and Pruitt's names in conversations, texts, and emails died in the avalanche, and he'd assign those identities to others. Not knowing whether Masterson was trying to protect his assets, the president put those names aside when he cleaned house, intending to take a closer look at them once he had a new FBI director.

Gao Hui's coffin left Zurich on a Chinese government aircraft three days later, the delay attributed to the government wanting to ensure that he received the proper honors upon his arrival in Beijing. Chien An accompanied him, writing the official report which stated he died in a car accident when his vehicle slid off an icy Swiss road and went over an embankment. The Nemesis team, out of respect, waited until the aircraft carrying his body departed before boarding the next flight to Dulles, which left six hours later.

When the aircraft carrying Gao Hui's body entered Chinese airspace, Air Force fighters escorted it to the Beijing airport, where inbound and outbound traffic was stopped until his plane touched down and taxied to the VIP terminal. President Liu and an honor guard met the aircraft and, after giving a televised speech about how Gao Hui had honorably served the people of China for decades and was a member of the Politburo Standing Committee, his coffin was taken by motorcade to the Babaoshan Revolutionary Cemetery, reserved for revolutionary heroes and high government officials, and cremated.

Cray was brought out of his medically induced coma when his brain scans returned to normal, indicating that his traumatic brain injury, caused by substantial blood loss, was temporary. Since the bullet didn't strike an organ, the doctor felt he could convalesce at home and cleared him to leave the hospital. However, the president had a different idea, insisting he stay at the White House residence, where he'd be under 24/7 observation by the White House physician and a rotating staff of nurses.

While at the residence, Cray kept informed on what was happening with the Nemesis team, including what Masterson told Moretti about his family being the sole buyer for generations of Helmand Province's poppy field extract and shooting down their helicopter to prevent him from signing an agreement that would destroy those fields.

"The DEA doesn't have anything on Tenant Masterson," the president said as the two spoke in the Solarium, which offered a panoramic view of the National Mall.

"I'm not surprised. In the years since my agreement in Helmand Province evaporated, I looked into who bought the sap from the poppy crops. Since the Afghans are better than the NSA at keeping secrets, I didn't get any traction. But I guarantee they know how to get ahold of Tenant Masterson, just as I know their code dictates that anyone telling an outsider their buyer's name forfeits their honor and life. I've experienced that firsthand," Cray said, explaining to the president what happened to the person who fired a weapon in violation of a truce the village elder ordered.

After telling this story, Cray became lost in thought, his concentration broken when the president asked if he was alright.

"Sir, would it be possible to use the vice-president's aircraft?"

With the help of President Ballinger, Cray asked the ambassador to Afghanistan to set up a meeting using the governor of Helmand Province as a go-between. However, the governor refused to meet when asked, saying his request would destroy the provincial farmer's trust in him. That position reversed when told that Cray was bringing a briefcase containing gold to compensate him for the inconvenience.

"How much gold?"

The ambassador gave the weight.

"The day after tomorrow," he said, giving the ambassador the location of the meeting.

The vice-president's aircraft was a modified Boeing 757, which made the six thousand nine hundred twenty-four-mile trip to Kabul in a little over twelve hours. Once it landed, Cray was escorted to a Chinook for the flight to Musa Qala in the same type and model of helicopter he and Moretti were in on his last visit to the province.

The landing was gentler than fourteen years earlier. Cray greeted the governor as he stepped onboard the aircraft and, shaking his hand, handed over the briefcase. After opening it and seeing the gold within, he led Cray to a mud-brick building nearly identical to the one destroyed on his last visit. He pointed to the door and walked away. Inside was the elder who'd previously granted him and Moretti pashtunwali, and the interpreter he'd used before.

"Salam alaykum," Cray said, meaning peace be upon you, placing his right hand over his heart as a sign of respect and denoting that the greeting was sincere.

The elder returned the greeting and gesture, inviting him for tea. Cray, who used a cane to take pressure off his wound, went to his chair.

"Did you have an accident?" the elder inquired.

Cray explained what happened at the airport.

"And you want to avenge this attack?" the elder asked.

Cray said he did, knowing the elder would understand and respect killing one's enemy and that vengeance wasn't unusual in Afghan culture.

"Because you're here, you must believe I know him."

Cray said that he was the buyer of the provincial poppy harvest and wanted to know his name.

"He'll be a formidable adversary."

"I know. But I need this favor."

The elder nodded, saying the farmers had sold his family their poppy sap for generations.

"How can I find him?"

"I don't know. Our agreement is that he pays cash upon the sap's delivery at the harvest's end. If he's late, we've told him we'd sell it to whoever pays us first. But, in generations, that's never happened. He sends huge helicopters towards the end of the harvest, the pilots and guards waiting for the farmers to finish producing the sap. Once we bag it, they weigh and load them into the aircraft. I'm told each helicopter can transport six thousand five hundred pounds."

"Where do they go?"

"I don't know."

Cray looked crestfallen. "I need to find Tenant Masterson," he said.

"We've sold the fruit of our crops to the same family since the middle of the eighteen hundreds, and their surname isn't Masterson."

"I understood that to be his name."

The elder shook his head and gave the name of their buyer. "Over the years, we've heard it used by those who transport our crops. The first name changes, but the family name remains the same."

Cray thanked him. "The president wishes to show his appreciation for your hospitality. Later today, helicopters will deliver medical supplies, generators, tools, and other items." Cray knew that giving cash would be an insult, but gifts didn't cross that line. This is my gift to you and your family," Cray continued, handing him the two satphones with chargers he removed from his jacket pockets. My direct dial number is in each. If you need my help, call."

"Khoda hafiz," the elder said, meaning that he hoped God would protect him.

Cray said goodbye by repeating what he'd heard and returned to his helicopter.

The Nemesis team landed in Dulles and were escorted through the VIP section of customs and immigration. Entering baggage claim, they saw three drivers holding signs. The one with Bonaquist's name had instructions to take him home. The driver with McGough and Shen's names would take them to their quarters at Site R. However, the driver for Moretti and Han Li went unnoticed because Jehona ran towards them. After a tearful reunion, they saw him and were led to a limo. When they got in, they were startled to see Cray.

"You're alive," Moretti exclaimed, drawing a laugh from Jehona and a look from Han Li that a wife gives a husband when he says something she couldn't believe came out of his mouth.

"From what I've been told, that's because the two of you had my back and saved my life a couple of times."

"You look great. What did the doctor say?" Han Li asked.

"Take a month off and relax while my wound heals."

"You're a workaholic with a type A personality, and you're incapable of either," Moretti responded.

"Agreed. Once I finished something I had to do, the president ordered me to get out of Washington for a month."

"Where are you going?" Moretti asked.

"Somewhere I've always wanted to go but never had time. The Amazon."

"You're in no shape," he responded. "We've both spent time in the jungle during our survival training. It looks tranquil on TV, but once you begin walking through this high-humidity environment, it quickly exhausts and dehydrates you. Also, everything in the jungle believes you're their next meal, and those with canes are the low-hanging fruit for these predators."

"I'm not walking; I'm sailing through it. This cane," Cray said, briefly lifting it off the seat for them to see, "will take the pressure off my wound as I stroll the deck."

"You're on a cruise ship?"

"A five-star river vessel called the Selva, which is the local word for jungle. I'll be looking at rainforests and some of the most beautiful scenery in the world. When I'm tired, I go to my five-hundred forty square feet air-conditioned suite on the upper deck or to one of two gourmet restaurants. The ship has a medical facility with 24/7 doctor care."

"Does it have three more staterooms?" Moretti inquired.

"No offense, but I prefer to go solo and not have two other persons with the same type A disorder accompanying me; Jehona is obviously the exception. Let me ask you this. In our job, how much time do we have to ourselves or a chance to travel for pleasure?"

"None," Moretti admitted.

"Will you be in the Amazon the entire month?" Han Li asked, deftly changing the subject.

"The cruise lasts eight days. It leaves from Manaus, which is in northwestern Brazil, and docks in Macapá on the Atlantic Ocean. From there, I'll fly to Rio and Buenos Aires, and how long I stay in each and where I go from there is open."

"When are you leaving?"

"In two hours," Cray answered. "The driver will take you to the vice-president's residence to spend the night. One more thing. I shared something with Alexson and Connelly that will interest you."

"Is that what you did before the president ordered you to take a vacation?"

"They've got the details," he said, ignoring the question and slowly getting out of the vehicle. As he was doing this, the driver removed a roller bag from the trunk and met him with it at the left passenger door.

Moretti, Han Li, and Jehona got out to say goodbye.

"Don't worry about Nemesis; we'll handle everything until you return," Han Li said.

"I don't doubt that for a second. If you need me, call my satphone. Otherwise, don't count on hearing from me."

"You might get bored being a tourist for thirty days," Moretti said.

"At least no one will try to kill me," he responded as he walked towards the terminal.

He was wrong.

At nine the following morning, the team assembled in the conference room at Site R, Moretti asking Alexson and Connely to join them. Both looked haggard.

"Cray said you had information to share with us," he said.

"Connelly and I have been working all night to pull as much data as we could before you got here," Alexson replied.

"Data on what?"

"Tenant Masterson."

"Where is he?" Moretti asked.

"In the Brookwood Cemetery in Surrey, England."

"You have the wrong Tenant Masterson. I saw this prick not long ago."

"Tenant Masterson's passport lists his date of birth as May 23rd, 1964. His passport application, which we got by hacking into a British government database, shows he was born in the village of

Betchworth, twenty miles from London, which has a population of less than a thousand. These specifics match the burial form for the person under a stone slab in Brookfield," Connelly explained.

Moretti felt the anger that was welling up within him. "That means we don't know who the thin man is."

"We do, thanks to Lieutenant Colonel Cray," Alexson said, detailing the trip to Helmand Province and his meeting with the elder.

"That was a brilliant move," Han Li volunteered.

"Who is he?" Moretti said, asking the question that was on everyone's mind.

"Harrison Carter."

"That could also be an alias," Bonaquist countered.

"The elder said that Carter's family has been working with the Helmand Province elders since the mid-eighteen hundreds."

"How do we find him?" Han Li asked

"That's the rub. It's a prevalent name. We wrote a program that will hack Britain's property and tax records and the Passport Office, which is part of the Home Office. Given how you earlier described him, we narrowed the search to those between the ages of forty and seventy. You'll still have quite a number of faces to look at."

"There may be an easier way," Moretti said. "We know that generations of his family have been in the military. Look at British army records for Harrison Carter and then search backward to see if previous generations of his family served in Afghanistan."

"Brilliant," Connelly said before he and Alexson left the room to hack British military records.

An hour later, they returned with a photo and a short dossier.

"Is this the person you saw in Davos?" Alexson asked, bringing in their laptop and showing Moretti and Han Li the image while Connelly distributed the dossier.

They both said it was the thin man, with the rest of the team confirming it was him.

"Now that we know his identity, it'll be hard for him to hide," McGough said.

"He's got the billions," Bonaquist countered as he scanned the dossier. "That's enough money to live in anonymity for the rest of his life. If he stays away from facial recognition security cameras networked to government databases, we've heard the last from him."

"For anyone else, I'd agree. But I think he has a score to settle. We know about his drug empire, leveled his home, and destroyed fifteen years of work and his life's ambition, which cost billions. He'll come after us, either as a group or individually, with everything he has."

He was entirely correct.

Harrison Carter was lounging on his pool deck in one of his Giorgetti Gea beach chairs, staring out at the tranquil waters of Raa Atoll. More than a decade ago, he'd purchased the private island on a detached reef at the northern end of the atoll to relax when he wanted to get off the grid. The island was in the Republic of Maldives, an archipelagic country in the Indian Ocean that was six hundred and ten miles off the coast of Sri Lanka. The non-extradition country was a haven for Russian oligarchs, the nefarious uber-rich, and those who wanted privacy without the worry of a foreign government seizing their assets or ordering their arrest and extradition for the misdeeds they were wholeheartedly guilty of committing.

His forty-thousand square feet atoll mansion was more luxurious than his home in Davos. It cost nearly twice as much to build because of its remoteness, which required everything to arrive by sea, and carried a heavy importation tax. Although communications and data links weren't issues because of his state-of-the-art satellite system, they lacked the privacy of the NSA's satellites. For that, he used Tor, short for The Onion Router. This encrypted and free, open-source software enabled anonymous communication by directing internet traffic through a worldwide system of six thousand relays that effectively concealed a user's location. Although what he sent and received would be recorded by the NSA, his location would remain unknown.

He was lucky to escape Switzerland. If the ambush near his residence focused on his vehicle instead of Kimmel's, his days of basking in the sun would be over. Instead, he could execute his escape plan and drive fifty miles to St. Gallen–Altenrhein Airport. En route, he confirmed the availability of a Falcon 50 jet charter based there. If it was gone, he had three other nearby airports with jet rentals.

Kimmel's escape route was different, involving a sixty-three-mile drive to an airport in Memmingen, Germany, where a plane would take him to London. There, he'd charter an aircraft to the United States, where he believed his ability to control the narrative on social media, along with a bevy of high-priced lawyers and his influence in Congress, would allow him to continue his business uninterrupted.

Carter knew he couldn't go nonstop to the Maldives because the Falcon only had a range of four thousand miles. But it would get him out of the country quickly. From St. Gallen–Altenrhein Airport, he flew thirty-five hundred miles to Doha, Qatar, where the aircraft refueled and continued another twenty-one hundred miles to the Malé International Airport, Maldives. Since he didn't have an airstrip on his island, he transferred to a helicopter for the one hundred fourteen-mile trip, smiling as he thought about the search for him throughout Switzerland and Europe. At the same time, he was thousands of miles away applying sunblock or dining on the local fish that his staff caught daily.

He was a planner and realist, knowing the Cabal was through because its key players were dead. Those who survived would eventually be compromised, either by Kimmel to save his hide or the NSA, after discovering the breach of their satellite system. If there was a silver lining, it was that the billions set aside to take them across the finish line were sitting in several offshore accounts to which only he had access. That would sustain his extravagant lifestyle and allow him to get even with those who destroyed his vision. The first person on that list was Cray, whose investigative persistence was responsible for the Cabal's demise and who he believed would be equally persistent in continuing his search for him.

Using Tor, he sent a message to Samuel Bradford asking if he knew where Cray went after leaving the hospital.

The FBI's executive assistant director for intelligence replied that he'd find out, later responding that he'd left the country and attaching his flight information to Manaus, the floatplane charter schedule, and his itinerary on the Selva.

After receiving it, Carter Googled the time difference between Manaus and the Maldives, finding the Brazilian city was nine hours behind him. Looking at his watch, he saw that Cray's Brazilian flight hadn't yet landed. He sent another message to Bradford.

"Do you have the means to take down his charter and ensure he doesn't survive?"

"I have someone in Brazil I've used in the past for wet work," Bradford replied, referring to the euphemism for murder that alludes to spilling blood. "He's particularly astute at taking down aircraft."

"Do it."

# AUTHOR'S NOTES

This is a work of fiction, and the characters within are not meant to depict nor implicate anyone in the actual world. Moreover, representations of corruption, illegal activities, and actions taken by government and industry officials were made for the sake of the storyline. They don't represent any illegality or nefarious activity by the persons who occupy or have occupied positions within government or industry. Substantial portions of *The Cabal*, as stated below, are factual.

One of the fun aspects of being a writer is dripping out the backgrounds of the central and supporting characters in successive novels, providing enhanced insight into their motivations and actions. To many, including myself, characters transcend their fictionality and take on a reality and life of their own. In this novel, you learned about the helicopter crash that ended Moretti's military career and how Cray saved his life. I also disclosed why Cray joined the military, his family background, why he became an Army Ranger, and how he ended up as an intelligence officer. These details will help you understand his capabilities and reactions to what I have planned for him in my next manuscript. It'll be a wild ride.

I often receive emails as to why I let characters die. Why can't everyone live? The reason is that a reader will never believe someone's life is in grave danger if, novel after novel, a character escapes a deadly situation because the author writes them out of it. Where is the edge-of-your-seat tension when you know they're going to live? There isn't any. Therefore, I've killed central and supporting characters, both loveable and scum, so you can never be sure who I'm going to ax next—if anyone. This means a character's danger is real, and they may not escape their situation.

The information on lobbying firms and the return on investment to corporations are accurate and taken from a 2022 article in *RepresentUs*. To repeat, lobbyists hired by corporations can legally raise money for those in Congress, whereas corporations cannot directly give money to them. Therefore, if a corporation wants to hand one hundred thousand dollars to someone in Congress, they hold a fundraiser. What usually follows is the lobbyist telling the Senator or Congressperson the name of the corporate entity behind the fundraiser and that additional events could be held depending on their position with future legislation. The article in *RepresentUs* provides an example from a *New York Times* article that reported that lobbyists for a major bank wrote seventy of the eighty-five lines of legislative language. This article, which names the bank and the legislation, can be found at (https://represent.us/action/5-facts-lobbyists/). This doesn't mean that all lobbyists operate in this fashion, but it does give you pause to wonder.

In my pre-writing research, I discovered that the Taliban make money through extortion, arbitrary taxation, and smuggling. For example, they've set up a toll system for trucks entering the country, a twenty percent zakat, or payment, on the sale of opium, and a tax on heroin labs. They have the support of farmers because, in the country's devasted economy, they put one thousand three hundred dollars a year in their pockets for growing opium poppy plants—a fortune by Afghan standards. Wheat, a far less profitable crop, is imported from Pakistan. With alternative livelihoods for farmers unavailable, it's doubtful that the government will eradicate poppy crops in Afghanistan. In 2020, it's believed the Taliban earned four hundred sixteen million dollars from the Afghan poppy economy, with forty-two percent of the world's opium coming from that country. You can find more information at

(https://www.brookings.edu/articles/pipe-dreams-the-taliban-and-drugs-from-the-1990s-into-its-new-regime/).

The British wanted to conquer Afghanistan to prevent the Russians from invading southward through its mountainous regions and into British India. These conflicts became known as the Anglo-Afghan Wars. During this invasion, opium was extracted from poppy plants and converted to morphine, codeine, and heroin. Heroin became mainstream in 1898 with its introduction by the Bayer Company in Eberfeld, Germany. However, studies showed that, when administered intravenously, patients became addicted to it. Subsequently, heroin became a prohibited drug. More information on this can be found in a January 1, 1953 article by the United Nations Office of Drugs and Crime, which is at

(https://www.unodc.org/unodc/en/data-and-analysis/bulletin/bulletin_1953-01-01_2_page004.html).

Information on the societal cost of heroin use disorder in the United States can be seen at

(https://www.ncbi.nlm.nih.gov/pmc/articles/PMC5448739/#:~:text=The%20estimated%20total%20cost%20of,Fig%202%3B%20S2%20Table)).

Afghanistan ranked one hundred-seventy-seventh out of one hundred eighty countries on Transparency International's corruption perception index. In 2014, General John R. Allen told the Senate Foreign Relations subcommittee: the existential threat to the long-term viability of modern Afghanistan is corruption and that insurgency, criminal patronage networks, and drug traffickers had formed an unholy alliance. You can find more information at

(https://en.wikipedia.org/wiki/Corruption_in_Afghanistan).

I took the description of Masterson's house in Davos, Switzerland, from a home in St. Moritz. If you want to look at this fantastic residence, replete with secret rooms, a wall covered from top to bottom with mink fur, and a breakfast nook and walk-in closets sheathed in 24-karat gold, go to (https://www. cnbc.com/2017/10/12/most-expensive-home-in-switzerland-is-on-the-market-for-185-million.html).

Soundproofing windows is generally done using thicker laminated glass and adding up to four inches of dead, sound-reducing air between the exterior and interior windows. These windows aren't cheap. A standard three-foot-by-five-foot soundproof window can run one thousand dollars; if the window size is non-standard, that cost can escalate to ten thousand dollars a window—without installation. For example, a homeowner in an airport flight path built a six thousand square feet custom home and paid two hundred fifty thousand dollars to install soundproof glass. In describing the thin man's mansion in Davos, I noted that his windows were bullet-resistant and soundproofed so the Cabal couldn't hear the howitzer sending explosive shells into the mountain slope above the mansion. You can find more information on soundproof glass at

(https://www.houselogic.com/remodel/windows-doors-and-floors/soundproof-windows/#:~:text=To%20increase%20 a%20window's%20ability,that%20further%20reduces%20 noise%20transmission).

A Faraday cage is an enclosure used to block electromagnetic fields. A December 2, 2021 article by Jonathan O'Callaghan in *LiveScience* and a May 8, 2015 article in *Engadget* by Mariella Moon explain Faraday cages. You can find these articles at (https://www. engadget.com/2015-05-08-faraday-cage-condo-san-francisco. html) and (https://www.livescience.com/what-is-a-faraday-cage).

Pashtunwali is a code of conduct by which the Pashtun people live and encompasses hospitality, sanctuary, righteousness, bravery, loyalty, courage, and honor. It dictates profound respect for all visitors, giving one asylum from their enemies at all costs. Marcus Lutrell's story, which became the movie *Lone Survivor*, provides an excellent example of Pashtunwali. A more detailed explanation can be found in an August 6, 2013 article by Yasmeen Aftab Ali in *The Nation*.

The StoneSprings hospital exists and provides extraordinary medical care. However, I've taken liberties with the interior description of the facility. Additionally, the hospital staff mentioned in this novel is fictional and doesn't represent past or present personnel working for or associated with the hospital.

The corruption within various offices and directorships of the CIA, DIA, FBI, and other federal agencies and institutions, along with those occupying positions within them, is fictional and was done for the storyline to illustrate the possibility that a longstanding independent bureaucracy could exist below that of elected officials. The Merriam-Webster dictionary defines this Deep State as *an alleged secret network of especially nonelected government officials and sometimes private entities (as in the financial services and defense industries) operating extralegally to influence and enact government policy*. Although it's generally acknowledged that the Deep State exists, I have no reason to believe that the agencies or individuals who occupy the positions mentioned in my novel are anything but honest and dedicated public servants.

Reference to members of the Skull and Bones society as a conspiratorial group engaging in illegalities is fictional and done for the sake of the storyline and is not based on fact or hearsay. No one knows much about this secret society and a host of others at educational institutions globally. What we know about the Skull and Bones society—also called The Order, Order 322, and The Brotherhood of Death is that it's an undergraduate senior secret student society formed at Yale in 1832. Its members are called Bonesmen or Members of the Order. Interestingly, The Order measures time five minutes out of sync with standard time, referring to the latter as barbarian time. Former and current members include George H.W. Bush, George W. Bush, John Kerry, Stephen Schwarzman (co-founder of The Blackstone

Group), Steven Mnuchin (former Secretary of the Treasury), and numerous senior government officials, ambassadors, captains of industry, and other influential members of society. Given the rumors surrounding The Order, I couldn't resist playing upon their secretiveness to strengthen the longstanding cohesiveness of the bad guys—Mea culpa.

A portion of the new world order's philosophy that I incorporated into the storyline came from a February 9, 2021 blog written by Carmen Celestini and published by H-Net Services. In this post, she speaks about the great reset conspiracy and the new world order (NWO), citing a video by Klaus Schwab, the founder of the World Economic Forum, in which he references the great reset and stakeholder capitalism where corporations are more than profit-making entities. In the NWO, corporations become societal trustees by paying higher taxes, instituting policies for environmental sustainability, and participating in a social welfare safety net. You can find this information at (https://networks.h-net.org/node/3911/blog/vistas/7252034/great-reset-conspiracy-covid-and-resistance).

I took the background information on the World Economic Forum and the World Social Forum from a 2018 *Institute for Global Dialogue* article, which you can find at (https://www.igd.org.za/infocus/65-wef-and-wsf).

The cost of attending the World Economic Forum is accurate, as are the methods of transport to it. I took this from a January 26, 2011 article by Henry Blodget in *Business Insider*, which can be found at (https://www.businessinsider.com/costs-of-davos-2011-1). Additional information on the WEF can be obtained from a January 24, 2011 article in the *New York Times* by Andrew Ross Sorkin at

(https://dealbook.nytimes.com/2011/01/24/a-hefty-price-for-entry-to-davos/).

Non-business participants in the WEF—such as heads of state and ministers from over seventy countries, leaders in the arts, and so on, do not pay. In addition, some in the academic community receive travel and funding. The Swiss government at the federal, cantonal, and municipal levels pick up the security tab. For further detail, there's a January 16, 2017 article by Oliver Cann, a former head of strategic communications and member of the World Economic Forum executive committee, which you can find at (https://www.weforum.org/agenda/2017/01/who-pays-for-davos/).

The Albanian mafia operates within Switzerland, although it's unknown whether they're in Davos. You can find the extent of their influence within the country in the following articles:

(https://en.wikipedia.org/wiki/Albanian_mafia) and

(https://www.swissinfo.ch/eng/ethnic-albanians-keep-a-grip-on-heroin-supply/679296).

The Molar Mic is manufactured by Sonitus Technologies and operates as described. The company is continuing to develop the system and, over time, hopes it will transmit the user's biometric data—including stress, exhaustion, and wound analysis. You can find more information on this system at (https://www.thedrive.com/the-war-zone/23517/the-pentagons-tiny-covert-mics-that-clip-onto-your-teeth-are-a-game-changer).

Smart contact lenses, also referred to as contact lens cameras, exist. Although a commercial version is not yet available—Samsung, Sony, and Google are all working on versions that provide augmented reality and the ability to make a video recording of everything the user sees. Samsung was issued a patent for smart contact lenses that snap a photo with a deliberate blink of the eye. Although neither DARPA nor the military has announced it's using this technology, articles suggest some form of it is being used or tested by the military and possibly agencies of the government. You can find additional information on this technology at

(https://www.fanaticalfuturist.com/2019/06/mission-impossible-style-smart-contact-lens-gets-us-militarys-attention/), (https://futurism.com/sonys-new-contact-lenses-let-record-store-everything-see), and (https://futurism.com/samsung-patents-smart-contact-lenses-built-camera).

The Cazis Tignez prison in Chur, Switzerland, is as represented and was built to replace a seventeenth-century incarceration facility with conditions that were less than desirable for both prisoners and staff. The new prison employs the Swiss concept that the purpose of incarceration is no longer to lock people away; instead, it's to prepare them for reintegration into society. To keep re-offending rates low, inmates are taught the skills and given the experience they'll need for this reintegration. The Cazis Tignez prison is bright and modern, its most significant design benefit being the amount of natural light and the view of the mountains. I took liberties in deciding to imprison both Moretti and Han Li there instead of sending Han Li to a woman's prison. You can find more information on the Cazis Tignez at (https://scale.jansen.com/en/themen/cazis-prison/).

Using an external magnifier such as a rifle scope, telescope, or binoculars to take pictures of things far away is called Digiscoping. The method for taking a photo through a rifle scope was obtained from a January 7, 2022 article by Robert Sparks in *OpticsMag* that went into more detail than was called for in the storyline. You can find this article at (https://opticsmag.com/can-you-take-photos-through-rifle-scope/).

As written, bulletproof glass isn't always bulletproof and is not solely glass. Instead, it's a combination of glass and plastic. Because nothing is entirely bulletproof, most industry experts use the term bullet-resistant. The resistance comes from the absorption of a bullet's energy. The thicker the glass, the higher the resistance.

There are ten levels of bullet-resistant glass. Level one can stop a nine mm round. Level ten can stop a .50 caliber Browning Machine Gun bullet. The two most common resins used to produce this "glass" are acrylic and polycarbonate plastics. Level one polycarbonate "glass" is one-quarter inch thick and can stop a round from an AK-47 or an M16. Increasing the thickness to one inch will stop a .357 magnum rifle bullet. When acrylic or polycarbonate is between two sheets of glass, it increases the weight to ten times that of a glass-only pane. Almost all bullet-resistance glass is vulnerable to a high-velocity round from a rifle. More information can be obtained by going to (https://www.armormax.com/blog/bulletproof-glass/) and

(https://www.wikihow.com/Break-Bulletproof-Glass).

The description of what happens to a bullet as it penetrates glass is accurate and taken from an article published by Hornady Law Enforcement & Military. You can find this at (https://www.hornadyle.com/resources/le-faq/what-can-i-expect-when-shooting-through-glass).

Having no idea how to hotwire a car because I have no mechanical or electrical skills beyond changing a light bulb or battery, I read several articles on how this could be done, primarily using a 2019 article in CarTreatments.com for my manuscript. Although calling AAA is the better option, if one is inclined to hotwire their vehicle, you can find this methodology at (https://cartreatments.com/steps-to-hotwire-a-car/).

I decided on an avalanche as my weapon of choice in wreaking havoc with the Cabal after reading a Natural Disaster Association paper on avalanches and their causes (https://www.n-d-a.org/avalanche.php). Given the novel's setting, this seemed a unique way to dispatch the bad guys. As I delved into how to make this happen, one thing led to another, and I discovered how avalanche-prone areas try to prevent "the big one" from occurring, which is how I learned about the Gazex system and 105 mm howitzers.

Information on the Gazex avalanche control system, which uses specially constructed exploder tubes and a propane-oxygen explosion to set off avalanches, is accurate and taken from a January 31, 2019 article by Vicki Gonzalez from KCRA 3 in Sacramento, CA and from an October 16, 2017 article by Lance Maggart in Ski-Hi News. You can find these at (https://www.kcra.com/article/cannons-avalanche-control-caltrans-gazex-echo-summit/26105932#) and (https://www.skyhinews.com/news/how-does-it-work-starting-an-avalanche-cdot-preps-gazex-avalanche-exploders-for-coming-winter-months/#:~:text=IS%20A%20GAZEX%3F-,Gazex%20is%20an%20avalanche%20control%20system%20that%20uses%20specially%20constructed,force%20from%20which%20triggers%20avalanches.).

The 105 mm howitzer is used in many avalanche-prone areas to alleviate unstable snowpack in lieu of employing the Gazex system or explosives such as TNT, PETN, RDX, ammonium nitrate, or nitroglycerin—which are either planted by hand or dropped from helicopters. The howitzer is a half-million-dollar weapon that is, as far as I know, leased from the Army. You can find more information on this avalanche-inducing weapon, including specifics used in my manuscript, at

(https://www.latimes.com/local/lanow/la-me-ln-mammoth-howitzer-20170108-story.html), (https://www.google.com/search?client=avast-a-3&q=weight+of+a+105+mm+M101A1+howitzer&oq=weight+of+a+105+mm+M101A1+howitzer&aqs=avast..69i64.3j0j7&ie=UTF-8), and

(https://www.army.mil/article/69294/new_ammunition_combines_four_artillery_cartridges_into_one).

A large avalanche can result in a million tons of snow cascading down a mountain at two hundred mph. This catastrophe occurs when layers of snow, referred to as snowpack, accumulate until it loses stability and breaks away from the slope. Avalanches are more prevalent than I thought. In the western United States, one hundred thousand occur each year. Worldwide, approximately one hundred fifty people die from this tragedy annually. I took the information on avalanches used in my manuscript from the National Geographic Resource Library. You can find this at

(https://www.nationalgeographic.org/encyclopedia/avalanche/print/).

The Institute for Snow and Avalanche Research, or SLF, exists and is headquartered in Davos, producing an avalanche bulletin twice daily during the winter. However, the howitzer in Davos is fictional and inserted for the sake of the storyline. Because my research couldn't determine whether the SLF has responsibility for the avalanche prevention measures described, I attributed it to them because it fit my narrative.

I took the information on the NSA's data center from a fascinating article by James Bamford that appeared in *Wired* magazine. The link to that article is below. The Utah Data Center (UDC) is a heavily fortified complex in Bluffdale, which sits in a bowl-shaped valley with the Wasatch mountain range to the east and the Oquirrh Mountains to the west. The UDC is believed to receive data from NRO satellites and cryptanalyzes or breaks unbelievably complex encryption systems employed by other governments and computer users who think they've downloaded an off-the-shelf encryption program that not even the NSA can break. Wrong! You can find additional information on this and the NSA at

(https://www.wired.com/2012/03/ff-nsadatacenter/#:~:text=10%20NSA%20headquarters%2C%20Fort%20Meade%2C%20Maryland%20Analysts%20here,also%20building%20an%20%24896%20million%20supercomputer%20center%20here).

A quantum computer is, on average, a hundred million times faster than a classical computer. Although it uses less power, it comes with challenges outlined in a paper by Bernard Marr. You can find this at

(https://bernardmarr.com/15-things-everyone-should-know-about-quantum-computing/#:~:text=Google%20announced%20it%20has%20a,content%20on%205%20million%20laptops.). Information on a quantum computer's ability to crack encryption is as described and taken from a May 24, 2021 article in *CNET* by Stephen Shankland. You can find this at (https://www.cnet.com/tech/computing/quantum-computers-could-crack-todays-encrypted-messages-thats-a-problem/).

The methods employed to protect printed circuit boards from being copied are accurate and taken from the website of Advanced Assembly, a company that offers PCB manufacturing and assembling services. You can find this at (https://aapcb.com/new-blog/protecting-your-electronic-product-from-copying/).

Although the Selva is a fictional ship, I took the description of its cruise from several Amazon cruises, including those at

(https://www.rainforestcruises.com/cruises/iberostar-grand-amazon?gclid=CjwKCAjwxZqSBhAHEiwASr9n9OnGXd byI5Nws2exJfcdAMYbACeruglKpp2sMgtiTA7kzrIK4P311 hoCLd4QAvD_BwE) and (https://www.nathab.com/south-america/amazon-river-cruise/?utm_source=google&utm_medium=cpc&utm_campaign=Search%20-%20Amazon&utm_term=amazon%20river%20cruises&gclid=CjwKCAjwi6WSBhA-EiwA6Niok0rBnGMxrUvza4L8wpveJVSJmZrOQpzNF3bOBJ9J1 h2B1Khkqv7TLBoCLTMQAvD_BwE).

Some might find it unusual that I used the word floatplane instead of seaplane, believing they're the same. While both can take off and land on any body of water, the fuselage or belly of a floatplane, which has floats or pontoons, does not contact the water. In contrast, seaplanes have a single hull and take off and land on their fuselage. For more information on these aircraft, go to a September 17, 2019 article by Alex Sanfilippo in *Twin Otter Blog & News*. You can find this at (https://teamjas.com/whats-the-difference-between-a-floatplane-and-a-seaplane/).

The Maldives is a tropical paradise of many white-beach islands surrounded by their lagoon. It has over five thousand coral reefs, each with diverse and beautiful marine life. Carter's mansion on Raa Atoll is fictional. The Alifushi and Etthingili islands, referred to as the Powell Islands on the Admiralty chart, comprise part of that atoll. Until the late 1990s, Raa atoll was off-limits to tourists. However, the government has changed this policy, and tourist resorts are now on the atoll's islands.

Tor, short for The Onion Router, is open-source software that provides online anonymity regarding the user's identity, location, and activity. Operating like a standard browser, it randomly directs its traffic through a network of global servers, wrapping it in several layers of encryption. Each relay only decrypts enough data to reveal the location of the previous and following relays. Every path is randomly generated, and none of the relays are recorded. Tor also deletes the user's browsing history and cookies after each session. You can find more information on this in *vpnMentor*, which is at (https://www.vpnmentor.com/blog/tor-browser-work-relate-using-vpn/).

The floatplane's takeoff procedures came from an interesting article by Dave Hirschman in the March 1, 2018 publication by the AOPA Foundation. You can find this at

(https://www.aopa.org/news-and-media/all-news/2018/march/flight-training-magazine/technique-water-takeoff).

# ACKNOWLEDGMENTS

Ed Houck, to whom this book is dedicated, is a good friend and ardent Matt Moretti-Han Li fan who told me that many times he'll read late into the night, not wanting to go to sleep without finding out how someone extracts themself from the latest predicament I've gotten them into. That's music to every author's ears. Ed's kindness, generosity, and thoughtfulness is the model for Vice-President Charles Houck.

To: Kerry Refkin, my pre-submission editor and muse. The incorporation of her suggestions, including story settings, was the glue for this manuscript.

To: Zhang Jingjie for her expert research. There's no one better at delving into a particular subject and providing the details that I require to sustain the authenticity of a situation. Thank you, Maria.

Go to alanrefkin.com for photos of me researching the many locations mentioned in my novels. *Story Settings* will let you see the referenced venues, weapons, aircraft, ships, etc.

# ABOUT THE AUTHOR

Alan Refkin has written eleven previous works of fiction. He is the co-author of four business books on China, for which he received Editor's Choice Awards for *The Wild Wild East* and *Piercing the Great Wall of Corporate China*. In addition to the Matt Moretti-Han Li action-adventure thrillers, he's written the Mauro Bruno detective series and Gunter Wayan private investigator novels. He and his wife Kerry live in southwest Florida, where he's working on his next Matt Moretti-Han Li novel, *The Chase*.

Printed in the United States
by Baker & Taylor Publisher Services